THE SERPENT SOCIETY

ALSO FROM JOE BOOKS

MARVEL AVENGERS

THE SERPENT SOCIETY

PAT SHAND

JOE BOOKS LTD

Published simultaneously in the United States and Canada
by Joe Books Ltd, 489 College Street, Toronto, ON M6G 1A5

www.joebooks.com

Library and Archives Canada Cataloguing in Publication
information is available upon request

ISBN 978-1-77275-208-3 (print)
ISBN 978-1-77275-209-0 (ebook)

First Joe Books edition: July 2017

Design: Sayre Street Books

Printed and bound in Canada
1 3 5 7 9 10 8 6 4 2

This one is for all of the creators who worked on the Avengers before me. I am honored to continue the stories of these heroes, and I remain in awe of all that you have done.

CHAPTER ONE

SLUG-RHINO-OCTOPUS

On the afternoon that would become known to the citizens of Bedford-Stuyvesant, Brooklyn, as "the Day the Sky Opened," Clint Barton was enjoying a late-summer barbecue with neighbors on the roof of his apartment building. Smoke rose into the air as Clint rolled the sausages on the grill, charring them up nice and crispy. He poked one with his skewer and looked at it, nodding with satisfaction. Carefully rolling the links off of the grill and onto a paper plate, which felt hot on his calloused hand, Clint shouted over his shoulder so his voice would carry over the music.

"Hey! S'ready! Help yourselves!"

Clint Barton may have not been the best choice to man the building's grill—that honor was held by the late Gilbert, a longtime renter whose unparalleled skill had earned him the nickname "Grills." But with Grills gone, Clint tried his best to honor the man's name by serving the good people of Bed-Stuy to the best of his abilities. It helped that he wasn't currently incapacitated by any extreme bodily injuries, which was unfortunately rare for him—a man tends to rack up quite a laundry list of injuries when spending his days using a bow and arrow to fight super-powered alien tyrants.

That was life as Hawkeye, though, and while it might not have been easy, it was just about the only thing that Clint knew he *was* the absolute best at.

Besides maybe Kate Bishop, but that was an entirely different story, and not something that Clint would admit to just anyone.

Clint grabbed himself a sausage, tossing it from hand to hand so he wouldn't burn himself. There were way more sausages than buns left, so he figured he'd let the others get the full experience, and bit into the bun-less meat. He nodded, frowning deeply in appreciation. "Not bad, Barton," he said aloud through smacking chews, wiping his hand on his jeans. "You've still got it."

Clint sat down on an overturned trash pail next to Janet and Emma, who were leaning against the ledge. Janet was a single mother, quiet but nice, and Emma was her freckle-faced, sandy-haired daughter, probably around eight or so.

To Clint, everyone who wasn't over twenty looked eight or so.

"You promised me a story!" Emma said with a wide grin, holding her hamburger with both hands.

"You're right, you're right. I did," Clint said. He took another bite of the sausage. "How's the burger? I did okay?"

Emma nodded. "Super good. STORY!"

"Right," Clint said. He leaned forward, elbow on knee, scruffy chin in his hand. "Riiiiight. Let's see . . ."

"Nothing crazy," Janet cut in. "Remember, whatever you tell Emma she's going to repeat to everyone in her class. I could do without Timothy Hopper's mom calling me up about her son having nightmares."

"No, nobody wants that. All right, so we're gonna have to Timothy Hopper-proof this," Clint said. "Classroom friendly, yet still adventurous, captivating . . ."

"Bloody!" Emma chimed in. "Mom lets me watch horror movies if I close my eyes when she says."

"Not bloody," Janet whispered.

"I think I've got one," Clint said, leaning in, the half-eaten sausage still in his grasp. He pointed the sausage at Emma and raised his brows over his crinkly eyes. "Have you ever heard of . . . *Oddball*?"

Clint was pretty sure that no one had ever delivered Oddball's name with the level of intensity he had just mustered up for this tale, but his was the only story Clint could think of that didn't have enough blood to earn Janet a furious call from Ms. Hopper.

Emma shook her head, her eyes gleaming.

"All right, so Oddball . . . he's a super villain," Clint said. Then he scrunched his face, reconsidering. "Okay, not so much *super*. Guy's a villain, let's just put it like that. He and I crossed paths a ways back. He was—get this—an evil juggler."

"Whaaat!" Emma cried.

Clint, feeding off of her reaction, continued. "Exactly what I thought. This freakin' . . . uh, guy, this freakin' guy, right, he has all of these balls—juggle balls, obviously, the guy juggles. These things were explosive, some had acid in 'em. Pretty much, he picked the last remaining villain gimmick and went for it, is what I'm thinking. So I rush into the fight, because what's a guy like Oddball gonna do to me, right? I'm an Avenger. Best archer in the world. So I come at him and his gang . . . and they're *way* better than I expect. I don't know how you can be a *good* evil juggler, but these guys—they're good."

"Whoa," Emma said. Her eyes had widened and she was looking up at the sky. Clint chuckled to himself, thinking that he was better with kids than anyone gave him credit for. Especially his exes.

"So they're hitting me with everything they've got, and I'm shooting their balls—the juggling balls—out of the sky. They're exploding, there's acid flying everywhere, smoke. It's a *mess*! And then—"

Emma dropped her burger. "*Whoa*," she repeated.

"You think that's crazy, wait for this next bit," Clint said, popping the last bit of sausage into his mouth. "Oddball reels back and—"

Emma pointed at the sky, terror flitting across her face. "Mommy!" she cried.

Clint, suddenly realizing that it wasn't his story garnering the reaction, turned around. He and his rooftop full of neighbors stared up at the sky above Bed-Stuy, which rippled violently with red bolts of lightning. The energy contracted and expanded disturbingly close to the building, moving rhythmically, almost like a heartbeat.

"Aww no," Clint muttered. He took a brief moment to mourn the loss of what had almost been an entirely peaceful day, and watched the energy expand in the sky, moving in and then out, growing then pulling back in what seemed to be a concentrated area. Clint sighed and stood on top of the overturned trash pail. He cupped his hands around his mouth as, around him, his neighbors began to panic.

New York might have been *the* hot spot for otherworldly activity, but that didn't mean New Yorkers were at all used to it.

"Everyone, listen up!" Clint called out. "Take your food inside, now! I'm going to find out what's up with the—"

"Is it an alien!?" Derrick from 2B called out.

"Are you gonna fight the alien!?" Rose from 4C cried.

A sound like a bomb going off rang through the neighborhood, silencing any further questions. A chorus of car alarms wailed below. Clint, attempting to see if the thunderous sound had produced anything from the sky, squinted up at the cluster of energy just in time to see the red lightning rip open a portal—being an Avenger, Clint knew portals, and *that* was a portal sure as any he'd ever seen—in the clouds. It wasn't apocalyptically sized, but it was big enough to fit a garbage truck or two.

Which meant that whatever was about to come out was probably *not* fun sized.

"Get in!" Clint shouted, waving people away. This time, they listened, though as they ran into the building the panicked chatter about aliens intensified.

Unfortunately for poor, scared Timothy Hopper, who would surely get all of the terrifying details, Emma was the last person into the building besides Clint. Pulled along by Janet, Emma looked over her shoulder just in time to see a pulsating, slimy, grey creature that looked like a deranged hybrid of a slug, an octopus, and a rhinoceros emerge from the portal, sending a wave of yellow slime smacking down to the street below, nearly dousing Clint in the noxious gunk.

"*Whoa,*" Clint and a horrified Emma said at the same time, right before Janet pulled her wide-eyed daughter into the building.

For a moment, Clint thought the creature—which wasn't quite as big as a garbage truck, but rather approximately the size of an obnoxiously large SUV—was going to fall to the ground and splatter over some poor cabdriver. But as soon as the creature began to dip in the sky, its back split open with a wet *smack*, producing a set of glistening, bony wings. It took flight, gliding with surprising speed past the building.

Clint had seen a lot in his life, but this was definitely the first time he'd seen one of *these*.

Just as he began to run down to his apartment for his bow and arrows, he heard another explosive *crack*, the same as the first. A flash of actual lightning shot across the sky, followed by an echoing boom of thunder.

That sound, Clint recognized.

Right before the rift closed and the red energy disappeared with a rippling effect, like water disturbed by a stone, the silhouette of a man far bigger than Clint flew out of the portal, in hot pursuit of the slug-octopus-rhino. Clint smirked.

"Hey, buddy," he said quietly.

As the silhouette tore through the sky like a bullet, heading right for the winged monster, Clint took off down the stairs leading back into the building. He knew that if he didn't hurry up, he'd miss a fight. And while he would've preferred to get through the barbecue without event, the Avenger in him just *had* to find out what was going on.

* * *

Thor Odinson—the Mighty Avenger, Asgardian God of Thunder, he alone who wields the enchanted hammer Mjolnir, and a bunch of other monikers that he'd have been happy to list off if he were in a better mood—shot through yet another portal in pursuit of the Barglewarf. He'd chased the creature through five of the nine realms over the better part of what would've otherwise been a glorious weekend celebrating some victory or other in Asgard's biggest banquet hall.

But no. He was on Barglewarf duty.

"Splendid," Thor said through gritted teeth, not for the first time, as he looked down and saw—he quickly scanned the area—the familiar neighborhood of Brooklyn, New York. After a bizarre journey through five portals, beginning in Asgard, the wayward beast had found its way to Thor's second home: Midgard. Or as the people of that world called it, "Earth."

He had been with Sif and the Warriors Three—his closest confidants, his greatest friends, and the four people he most enjoyed showing up. They were warding off a group of Barglewarfs—which were quick and vicious beasts to be sure, but normally no great threat—driving them away from Asgard. A herd had come too close to the kingdom, and the warriors knew that if one of the creatures got in, the stench of its slime would take millennia to remove. They'd delayed the start of their weekend plans in order to lure the monsters away, but Thor had broken off when the biggest and nastiest of the pack had made a beeline back to the kingdom. Just as Thor had caught up with the rogue Barglewarf, a rift had opened in the sky before him, and the foul beast had galloped right through it.

While even the foolhardiest soul in Asgard would advise against blindly flying into a portal, Thor glimpsed the land that lay beyond the rift and recognized it as Jotunheim, the world of the Frost Giants. If a destructive Asgardian creature like a Barglewarf were to make its way into that world, it would be seen an act of aggression toward the Frost Giants, who were always ready to go to war with Asgard at the slightest perceived infraction.

So, Thor followed the Barglewarf into Jotunheim.

And then, Thor followed the Barglewarf through *another* portal into Alfheim.

And another portal into Muspelheim.

And another portal into Svartalfheim.

And now the Barglewarf was flying through Brooklyn, raining its vile slime over shocked New Yorkers who, while used to pigeon droppings raining from the sky, were not quite prepared for this particular brand of Asgardian excrement.

Thor had no idea who was opening these portals or why, but he was beyond done with this wretched Barglewarf. It was tireless, and the energy of the portals excited the vile thing, making it move even faster. Most of the denizens of the Nine Realms would be able to fend for themselves, but the amount of damage a hyper Barglewarf could do on Earth, especially in a place as densely populated as Brooklyn, was disconcerting to say the least.

Besides, Thor thought as he blasted after the creature, storm clouds building above him as he twirled his mighty hammer until it was a blur of gleaming Uru above his hand, *if I manage to slay the accursed beast soon, perhaps there will be time to put together a victory banquet after all!* He could recount the tale of the cross-dimensional chase, and drink to his magnificent triumph.

Now, he just had to work on the triumphing.

As the blurring hammer began to spark with dazzling veins of electricity, Thor's mane of blond hair was thrown back. Wind picked up around him as he created a storm from thin air, channeling it all into his hammer. His bright blue eyes matched the color of the electricity, and his shining armor gleamed as his hammer glowed in a spinning orb of light above him.

Finally, Thor tossed Mjolnir at the Barglewarf as the beast dipped closer to the street, careening toward people abandoning their cars to flee the monster. The Barglewarf shot up and curved around as Mjolnir rocketed past it— but Thor already had his hand held out, calling the hammer back to him. Faster than even his speedy, slimy opponent could comprehend, Mjolnir was back in Thor's grasp and ready for another strike.

Just as the Barglewarf arced back in a different direction, Thor held the hammer to the sky, channeling a hurricane's worth of lightning into its Asgardian metal. Before he could throw Mjolnir, which now glowed white hot with power, Thor saw an arrow zip past him and lodge in the Barglewarf's head, right behind its ear.

Floating in midair, the God of Thunder lowered the hammer, his red cape whipping around him.

"Barton?" Thor questioned aloud, with the air of a dude running into an old frat buddy at a bar.

The arrow exploded, sending the Barglewarf spiraling downward. It smacked into an apartment building and began to slide down the brick, leaving a thick, bubbling trail of slime.

"Barton," Thor said with a toothy grin. This time it wasn't a question.

Thor flew toward the fallen creature and, sure enough, saw Hawkeye—out of costume in a purple T-shirt and a pair of dirty jeans—perched on a fire escape, reaching into his quiver. He saluted Thor as the Asgardian Avenger flew past.

"Meet ya there," Clint said, and pulled an arrow with a thick cord attached to the end of it into his bow.

"Aye," Thor said, his eyes locked on the Barglewarf, which was limping away from the building, the skin on the back of its head bubbling where the arrow had detonated.

As Thor landed in front of the creature, Clint shot the specialized arrow into the slime-covered building, a long cord stretching from the arrow's shaft back to the bow. Its tip drilled into the brick with a high-pitched whine and anchored there, allowing Clint to jump off of his fire escape and swing down on the cord. He landed next to Thor, and the two stared down at the Barglewarf, which looked at them with growing, animalistic rage, its breath ragged.

"Friend of yours?" Clint asked, nocking another arrow in his bow.

Thor lifted his hammer just as the Barglewarf prepared to take flight again.

"Acquaintance," Thor corrected, and delivered a mighty blow to the monster's head. Lightning flowed into the creature's body and it writhed while Thor summoned more, illuminating the entire block.

Clint shielded his eyes. "Show-off."

The Barglewarf lit up with white light as Thor pumped it with lightning, and then, after one more weak attempt to escape, it collapsed in front of them, letting out one final moan. Thor pulled back his hammer and stared at the creature's corpse with satisfaction.

And then it exploded in a surge of hot, yellow slime, drenching both Thor and Hawkeye from head to toe.

Hawkeye, the goo dripping off of him in heavy clumps, turned to Thor and lowered his bow. "Could've let me shoot it. Reeaaally could've just let me shoot it."

Thor stood proudly over the steaming remains of the creature, unfazed by the coating of slime that hung heavily in his long hair and beard. "No, my friend. This battle was *mine* to finish."

Clint stared at Thor, deadpan. " . . . Your grudge against that slug-rhino-octopus was worth this?"

"Barglewarf. And *oh*, indeed it was." Thor slapped Clint on the back. "You live around here, yes? It was I who saved the day, so I believe that earns me first dibs on your shower."

CHAPTER TWO

OFF DUTY

Steve Rogers had to admit that he saw the benefit of texting, but, truth be told, he missed the days when people picked up the phone and called one another when they needed to talk. When Rogers felt his cell phone buzz in the left side of his utility belt—that side meant Avengers business—he was in the midst of a hostage situation at the Brantwood Bank, just a few blocks away from his apartment.

Steve had been on his way to cash a check when he found the door to the bank locked. He had been about to turn away, but then noticed that, according to the plastic sign listing the hours, the bank should be open. When he looked in, he saw a guy dressed in black standing while everyone else was on the floor.

He proceeded to tuck the check into his pocket and, clenching his thick bicep, slammed his shoulder into the locked door, sending the dead bolt skittering across the ground like a discarded coin.

Then, very casually, he had walked into the bank.

Which brought him to now. The phone buzzing in his

pocket almost always brought bad news—usually stuff far worse than bank robberies. Stuff such as time-traveling warlord Kang the Conqueror threatening to destroy reality as he battled his future self, or robotic sociopath Ultron creating an army big enough to fill up an entire country, or an entire prison of super villains coordinating a mass breakout. That kind of thing.

Whatever it was this time, though, it had to wait while he dealt with the man in black, who was staring at him incredulously, aiming a semiautomatic shotgun at Rogers with his right hand while he held a bank teller by the back of the neck with his left. All around the marble room, civilians and employees alike knelt on the floor, every bit as shocked to see the man they all recognized as Captain America as the bank robber was. The only other person standing was a trembling old man behind the help desk, separated from the situation by a thick pane of bulletproof glass. He had been fumbling with a set of keys, seemingly about to give the masked man the money he was asking for in exchange for the other teller's life.

Steve held a hand up to him and gave a slight shake of his head. The man instantly stopped.

The robber squinted at Steve, as if he didn't believe what he was seeing. "You're . . . you're . . . you're *Captain America*."

Steve strode toward the bank robber, whose eyes were wide behind the holes of his ski mask, which Rogers could tell had been hastily cut out with scissors. This guy wasn't pro. He didn't even have time to buy a proper ski mask, nor was he wearing gloves. And the hand holding the gun shook.

"I'm off duty," Steve said, gesturing to his outfit. He wore a grey shirt, which clung to his muscles, a pair of faded blue jeans, and running shoes. If he weren't nearly as brawny as Thor and a head taller than anyone in the room, he might have been just another guy in the bank. "You can call me Steve."

The robber had every right to be shocked. It wasn't every day that Steve Rogers, the famed Captain America himself, took on of a run-of-the-mill bank robber. Captain America was a legend.

Everyone knew the story. When Steve Rogers had attempted to join the ranks of the army during World War II, he was deemed unfit. Too frail. Sickly. Weak. However, when he proved to the United States of America that he had the heart of a soldier, they used him as a test subject for the super-soldier serum, which turned him into the hero he was today: Captain America. He fought alongside the United States Armed Forces as both a soldier and a symbol of the American ideals of hope, freedom, and the pursuit of happiness. He became a war hero. But when the war ended, Captain America was missing and presumed dead, until he was uncovered frozen in a block of ice, but alive. Steve Rogers emerged into a new world where he would once again take up the mantle of Captain America, fighting alongside the Avengers against the most powerful super villains the universe had to offer.

So no, he wasn't quite the person you'd expect to show up to stop a bank robbery.

"St-Steve?" the robber stammered out.

"Yeah. What's your name?" Cap asked.

Shaking his head, as if waking up from a dream, the robber let out a panicked laugh, which sounded more like a squeal. "Hey. I-I'm not falling for this. Don't get any closer, man," he said, shaking the gun at Steve. Then he pointed it down at the teller, who closed her eyes, her lips moving silently in what Steve knew was prayer. "Y-you don't want her to die, do you?"

"No one's going to die, son," Steve said. "How old are you?"

"What's it matter?" the robber snapped. "Huh? What are you doing here, anyway? What, does the government have this place on surveillance? Has Big Brother tapped into the cameras?"

Steve eyed the room. There were two stations set up with deposit slips and pens, which were attached to the platform with foot-long chains. One of them was closer to the robber, which Steve didn't want to risk. The other was just a few yards across the room.

"I came here to deposit a check," Steve said, turning

away from the robber. He walked slowly to the far platform, attempting to be as casual as could be. "Turns out, you just picked the wrong bank. No one here even got the chance to call the cops. In fact, I passed a police officer on the corner. He was petting someone's dog."

"Get out of here," the robber said, shoving the gun toward the woman's head and pressing its muzzle against her temple. "Now."

Steve stood in front of the signing station and turned around. He leaned slightly back against it, propping his elbows up on its surface. Casual, calm.

"How much did you ask them to give you?" Steve asked.

"I said *GO!*"

Steve slowly reached his fingers back until he felt the cool metal of the chain. He began to gather it up in his hand.

"How much?" Steve said. "Look at me. I don't have my uniform. No shield. No weapons. All I've got in my pocket is that check I came here to deposit. How *much*?"

"S-seventeen thousand, five hundred," the robber said, his voice hitching on the word ". . . thousand."

"That's one specific number," Steve said. "You in debt? Student loans?"

"Not me," the robber said, his eyes set in a glare behind the ski mask. "My father. He . . ."

His eyes fell to Steve's hand just as the hero clenched his fist around the thin metal chain and ripped it out of the platform. The robber, instantly panicking, pointed the gun at Steve, holding it now with both hands. The teller ran off to the side, scrambling away. Before the masked man could shoot, Steve, in one fluid motion, pitched the pen and the chain at the robber. Just as the would-be thief's finger was pressing the trigger, the pen whistled toward him like a rocket and stuck into his bare wrist, the chain following behind it, lashing across his hand.

The robber, stunned, dropped the gun to shake the pen out of his flesh, but Steve was already running at him. He grabbed the gun right before it would have clattered onto the marble floor, which could've triggered a shot. With his other hand, he shot his open palm into the robber's chest, taking him off his feet with the force of the blow. Steve snapped the gun over his knee and shells rained down onto the floor.

As he knelt down next to the fallen robber, who was gasping for air, he felt his Avengers cell phone buzz again.

Steve pinned his knee in the robber's chest as the entire room full of hostages cheered. Waving them off, Steve looked down at the masked man's wide, gleaming eyes. He reached under the cloth of the ski mask and pulled it upward, revealing the man's face. He was young and full-faced, maybe twenty, twenty-one years old. A mop of brown hair. Tears flowing from his eyes.

"Your father," Steve said, plucking the pen's tip from the robber's wrist. A thin river of blood flowed out. Cap tied the ski mask around the wound. "What happened to him that he needs exactly seventeen thousand, five hundred dollars?"

"I think . . ." the robber gasped, sucking in air, "I think I'm dying."

"You just have the wind knocked out of you," Steve said, loosening his knee on the man's chest. "Take a second. Deep, slow breaths."

After the robber could breathe regularly again, he told Steve everything. His mother was going through surgery, and without insurance, they couldn't afford treatment. His father, desperate to help, had tried acquiring a loan the legal way, but it hadn't worked out, which led him to a danger-ous alternative. He now owed a local gangster, Paulie Chase, seventeen thousand five hundred dollars. He'd already come up late once, and had paid with a finger. Today, it would be a hand. The next day, his life.

"I couldn't let him die," the robber said. To Steve, he no longer looked like a grown man. He was just a kid. "I couldn't . . ."

"This wasn't the answer," Steve said. He looked up and saw a pair of policemen enter the bank. He inclined his head, signaling them over. "What's your father's name?"

"Albert Matarazzo. Wh-what are you gonna do?"

Steve held his gaze for a beat, and then stood. The police-men pulled the young man up by the arms, and Steve, unable to help himself, said, "Not too rough."

Walking away, Steve made awkward eye contact with the elderly teller behind the glass, who was still trembling. For a moment, he considered walking up to the old timer and asking if he could go ahead and deposit his check, but he decided that it'd better wait.

Once outside, he pulled out his phone and saw two text messages, both of them from Tony Stark.

The first one read: *Steve. Avengers Tower, 8 p.m. Possible situation. Barton and Thor are rallying the troops. Could be a thing.*

The second one: *Your turn to bring snacks.*

Steve looked at his phone. 4:30 p.m. Three and a half hours. The perfect amount of time.

After texting Tony *I will be there*, Steve pulled up his contacts and selected Natasha Romanova. He put the phone to his ear. She picked up after six rings.

"Hi, Steve," she said. "I think you might be the only person who still calls me."

"What do you mean?"

"Gotta learn to text, buddy," she said.

"I know how to text," he said. "I just texted Tony."

"I figured that's what you were calling about. Are you going to make it tonight?" she asked.

"Of course," he said. "Aren't you?"

"I was about to grab a jet out to Moldova. I got a heads-up on a possible location for that arms dealer I mentioned," she said. "I tried to call Tony to get more details, but he didn't pick up. You think this is serious?"

"Tony said it could be 'a thing.'"

"I got the same text," she said with a sigh. "I could send someone else to Moldova. I have people close enough. I just really wanted to bust this guy myself."

"If you have time before eight, I've got a local guy in need of some busting," Steve said.

"Always have time for a good bust. What's the name?"

Steve watched as the police officers ushered the young man out of the bank toward the back of their squad car. He lowered his voice, and said the name into the phone.

"Paulie Chase."

"Oh, I know Paulie Chase," Natasha said. "*Please* tell me we have enough to take him down."

"Maybe," Steve said. "First, I need you to head over to his place. I just had a kid over here saying . . . well, it doesn't matter. I have to go make a stop. There's a guy who might be getting his hand cut off by Paulie if I don't find him first."

"Got it," Natasha said. "So you'll find the guy—fingers crossed, still with a pair of hands—and I'll check Paulie's place."

"As soon as my guy is safe and in hiding, I'll meet you there," Steve said. "Keep me updated."

"Widow out."

* * *

Natasha Romanova, better known to the criminal underground as the Black Widow was, unlike Steve Rogers, dressed for business.

Her black jumpsuit was one with the shadows of the evening as she crept through the darkness in front of Paulie Chase's Park Avenue mansion—a disgustingly arrogant display of wealth earned through bullying, extortion, and murder—getting the full scope of the place before picking her entry point. It was gated, and there were cameras, but Natasha had tools to solve both of those problems. She had been trained as an elite spy and deadly assassin in the Soviet Union's Black Widow Ops Program and later, upon taking her skills to the United States, found herself clashing with the Avengers. Clint Barton had shown her the error of her ways and had helped her sever her ties with the organization that had sought to turn her into a weapon. Ever since then, she fought alongside of him as an Avenger.

Black Widow settled on a particularly shadowy area next to a pillar upon which sat a stone gargoyle. It looked up at the moonless night sky, its mouth open in a silent roar, displaying four stubby teeth.

"Tacky," Natasha said, pulling a small cylinder out of her belt. It was no bigger than a tube of lipstick or one of those lasers people used to drive their cats crazy. She had a fair share of her own high-tech devices, but this one had been a gift from Tony Stark, which made it unique. The man might have his problems, but if there was one thing he knew, it was how to give the perfect gift.

Natasha pressed the smallest button on the tube, slowly sweeping it in an arc around Chase's property. Then she held down the bigger button for five solid seconds. The device gave a slight, almost undetectable chirp, letting her know it was successfully activated.

In the past, she may have sent off a minor electromagnetic pulse to disable the cameras, but that would possibly alert Chase and whoever else was inside to her arrival. Tony had designed this device—which he called "The Side Eye"—to essentially repel security cameras. Once activated, the device acquired the location of all nearby cameras and then remotely made every camera within a twenty-yard radius rotate *away* from the device. So as Natasha scaled Paulie Chase's fence, nimbly climbing the bars and throwing herself onto the other side of his property without so much as rustling the grass, the cameras repositioned themselves, turning away from her as she dashed across the lawn.

There was a sports car in the driveway, but Natasha knew that didn't necessarily mean the man was home; he seemed like the sort of guy who owned ten sports cars. However, she did glimpse the soft, blue glow of a television coming from inside the largest window on the side of the house. She sneaked through the bushes, remaining low to the ground.

Once she had a better angle, she knelt to the side of Chase's flagpole and pulled out a set of miniature, mechanized binoculars equipped with night vision. They fit onto her face like a pair of glasses. Brushing a lock of red hair out of the way, she tapped the side of the binoculars, zooming in on the window.

The glow was indeed from the television, and a balding, shiny head faced away from Natasha, toward the screen. She recognized the greased scalp as Paulie Chase's. She scanned every other visible window with her binoculars, and found that Paulie was, as far as she could tell, alone.

Paulie Chase wasn't quite as notorious as other New York mobsters, such Wilson Fisk, or Mister Negative. But he was Maggia affiliated, and ran what the Avengers suspected was a New York branch of Count Luchino Nefaria's crime empire. Neither the Avengers nor the police had been able to pin any specific crimes on him, but if Cap's intel was good, they might finally have something that could lead to charges. If they could bring him down, and save a man's hand from getting lopped off at the same time, it was a good night indeed.

She knew that Captain America wanted her to wait before making a move. In fact, he'd made her promise, warning her that Paulie Chase had the potential to be a far more dangerous adversary than they imagined. There had been persistent rumors that Paulie Chase had super powers. Nothing substantiated, though—just reports here and there of something unexplainable happening during police and gang run-ins. Because of this possible complication, Black Widow's goal was merely to get a visual on Paulie while Cap got his target to safety, but, as time passed and it became clear that Cap was taking his sweet time getting there, she grew bored. Besides, there seemed to be very little that was less threatening than the gleaming head in front of that TV.

She was going in.

Black Widow approached the door, wondering if *now* was a good time for an EMP. A gangster at Chase's level surely had a security system, so she couldn't just pick the lock and enter without him knowing. She'd lose the element of surprise with the EMP, but the door was close enough to Chase's location that he would hardly be able to make it off the couch before she'd be on him.

A sliver of light emanated from the side of the door, vertically. Narrowing her eyes, Black Widow inched forward, surprised to see that the door was ajar. Slowly but steadily, as to not produce a creak, Widow pushed it open with her black boot and stepped into the house, one hand gripping her pistol, the other, her baton.

She preferred to use the latter, but wouldn't hesitate to resort to the former.

But she wouldn't have to. Chase didn't move when she entered the room, nor when she, the gun trained on him, circled around to the front of the couch. His jaw was slack and the glow of the television reflected a warped pattern of colors on the puddle of blood spread beneath him on the leather couch.

"Natasha . . ."

Black Widow pivoted to the left, pointing her gun at the silhouette entering the room.

Steve Rogers, eyes wide, raised his hands instantly. "It's me," he said.

Letting out a long breath, Natasha holstered the gun and her baton. Cap circled the room, looking at Paulie Chase's body with distaste. There was a large puncture wound in the neck, but Natasha could tell it wasn't from a gunshot. He'd been stabbed by something thick, something cylindrical.

Cap met Natasha's gaze. "You didn't . . ."

"*No*," Natasha said with a scoff. "Are you kidding me?"

"I have to ask," Cap said. "He could've attacked. And with the Nefaria connection, there's always the chance those rumors about his powers are actually true. You could've had to—"

"I didn't," Natasha cut in. She pulled her glove off, then held the back side of her hand against Chase's face for a moment. "He's been like this over an hour. Could that kid's dad have done it himself?"

"No," Cap said. "I checked on him before I left. Gave him and his wife enough money to hole up in a motel while we . . ." He gestured to the body, shaking his head. "Took care of *this*."

"Saint Rogers," Black Widow said.

Steve didn't reply.

"This wound is strange," Widow said, taking a closer look at Chase's neck. "I'd say ice pick, maybe."

"Maybe. I'm wondering if this comes from within the Maggia or if it's another gang acting out," Cap said. "We'll let the NYPD know, but we'd better keep an eye on this. If the Maggia is on the brink of a gang war in New York, that spells trouble for everyone."

Widow turned to Cap, narrowing her eyes to slits. "You really thought I would've just killed this guy on his couch?"

Cap smiled, but it faltered quickly. "No, I—listen, if he went to shoot, I know you would've been quicker. That's all I'm saying. I wasn't accusing, I was just asking."

Widow nodded. "Well. This was maybe the most morbid bust of my life. Thanks for that, Steve."

Cap raised his brows. "Yeah. Not fun."

After Cap called the police and alerted them to the situation, the two of them hopped onto Black Widow's motorcycle and headed off to Avengers Tower in silence, both unnerved by what they had just seen, and both unwilling to talk about it.

CHAPTER THREE

GLOWY FINGERS

Captain America and Black Widow were the last to arrive at Stark Tower. As they emerged from the elevator into the penthouse, the voice of F.R.I.D.A.Y., Tony Stark's artificial intelligence that operated his Iron Man suit and all other devices tied to the same network, spoke to them in a chipper, welcoming voice.

"Welcome, Steve. Natasha."

"Hi, F.R.I.D.A.Y.," Natasha replied, as Steve offered an awkward half smile. There were many things he'd caught on to living in the modern age, but having a casual interaction with an AI's disembodied voice wasn't one of them.

They walked into the main area of the room, which was—in true Tony Stark fashion—excessive in its elegance. Italian-leather couches, tables made from glass and that looked more like modern art than furniture, and the softest plush carpet in all of New York City. The room spread out around them in a 360-degree view around a kitchenette and a game room, and was surrounded by tempered-glass windows that spanned the circumference of the penthouse.

Clint, padding barefoot across the floor, popped the top off of a beer bottle and flicked the cap over his shoulder and onto the carpet. He inclined the beer toward Steve and Natasha. "Hey hey."

"God, Barton, you smell like a skunk," Natasha said, cringing as she crossed his path.

Clint snickered and sank down onto the couch next to Bruce Banner. Banner, a kind-looking man with a soft smile on his face and a distant look in his eyes, was dressed in a violet button-up shirt and grey dress slacks. As Clint leaned toward him, a devilish grin plastered on his face, Banner's kindly expression soured. That made Clint laugh even harder.

"What can I say? I showered. Thor said the stink could last for days. That's not a problem, is it?" Clint put his arm around Banner, who stood, leaving his fellow Avenger alone on the couch, cackling. Behind him, Thor, wearing a T-shirt so tight across his broad chest that it threatened to rip, grinned widely as well.

"You should double check that you're not infected," Banner said, running a hand through his salt-and-pepper hair, still wincing from the odor. "That . . . that is rank."

"Where's Tony?" Steve asked, setting his bag of groceries down on the table. Clint reached in and grabbed a bag of chips, which he opened and began munching on.

Banner pointed downward. "Deep in the belly of the

beast. He was working on something when we got here. He'll be up any . . . hour now."

Bruce Banner may have been joking, but Steve knew there were few people who understood Tony Stark's obsession with work the way Banner did. Before Banner became an Avenger, he had been one of the top scientists working for the United States military, supervising the creation of a gamma-ray bomb. During a trial run that went awry, he'd been exposed to a massive amount of gamma radiation, which every one of his peers believed would kill him. Bruce Banner didn't die, though. Instead, something was born inside of him: the Hulk. A deadly and seemingly invulnerable monster with an unquenchable appetite for destruction and a mighty rage, the Hulk was an overgrown Mr. Hyde to Bruce's mild-mannered Dr. Jekyll. Though the creature had seemed uncontrollable, with practice, Banner had found that it was like any other curiosity of science: in the wrong hands, it could be an instrument of evil, but by regulating the beast within, it had the potential to be an incredible force of good.

In Hulk form, Banner's strength was on par with Thor's. However, what made him an incredibly valuable asset to the Avengers, beyond the Hulk's ability to smash even the most powerful villains that crossed them, was Banner's immense intellect and childlike sense of curiosity. If he and Tony began speculating, they could spend days lost in the process together, bouncing around ideas, debating process, and challenging each other in ways only they were able to. However, that was a rare event. Banner understood something very simple about Tony Stark, something that he didn't think the other Avengers were aware of: no matter how much of a riot Tony could be, being a man who looks at the world and asks *what if* was a solitary pursuit. Even when Tony Stark and Bruce Banner were in a room full of people, part of them—the most essential part, perhaps—was alone, pondering that question.

Steve sat on the couch next to Clint, seemingly unfazed by his odor. Clint offered him the open bag of chips, from which he took a handful. When he was done, he passed the bag to Thor, who accepted it with his gigantic hand.

"Ah, barbecue," Thor said, reaching in, and with a massive grab, leaving nothing but crumbs at the bottom of the bag. "Delicious. Excellent choice, Cap. Everyone is fond of barbecue."

"Everyone, huh?" Widow said, peering over his shoulder into the nearly empty bag.

"I'm going to guess that the reason you two stink is related to this meeting," Steve said. "But Thor . . . I have to ask. What's with the shirt? Is that an extra small?"

"Oh, that tiny tiny shirt?" Tony Stark's voice sounded from across the room. Dressed in sweatpants and a vintage black Led Zeppelin shirt, the sleeves rolled up to his elbows, he walked out of the elevator. F.R.I.D.A.Y. offered him a welcome, which he waved off. He treaded over to the others, wiping what appeared to be motor oil from his hands onto his pants. "You didn't hear? Thor's joining a boy band. The Odinsons. Sort of a new-wave hair-metal thing. While I'm not personally fond of their sound, I can definitely see them finding an audience. All in time."

Thor picked at the neck of his shirt. "This belongs to Barton. My garments are being soaked to remove the putrid stench of the Barglewarf that we slew this day," he said. Then, with a devious grin, he leaned in to the others and put his hands on Clint's shoulders. "It is a very small shirt for a very small man."

"Bull," Clint said, sending a few playful elbows back at Thor. "It's a medium. For a, uh . . . a medium-to-large kind of guy."

"Can someone write down that Clint just said that?" Natasha asked, crossing her legs. "I really, *really* want to remember that."

"Hey," Clint said, shrugging. "I'm not trying to impress anyone. I killed a slug-rhino-octopus today, so as far as I'm concerned, I'm pretty much the man."

"*We* slaughtered the beast," Thor corrected. "Mostly me."

"One could argue that," Clint said, "but one would be wrong."

"Wait, wait, wait, hold the bickering. Are . . . are we meeting today because of a . . . a 'slug-octopus-rhino,' that was?" Tony asked, opening a bag of tortilla chips. He popped one into his mouth, chewing it as he paced the room, eyes narrowed. "Is that ridiculous thing you just said the reason why my latest Iron Man suit is down in the lab, alone? Lonely? Without my tender caress? And, hey, also, Cap—no barbecue? Come on, man. You were on snack duty. Where's the sense of responsibility here?"

Cap pointed a thumb back at Thor. "Ask the man in the tight shirt."

Thor licked the orange chip dust off of his fingers. "Everyone likes barbecue."

"Can we go back to slug-octopus . . . what was the last part?" Banner asked. "I'm attempting to work up a mental picture here."

"Slug-*rhino*-octopus," Clint said. "Big guy. Real nasty. Somehow, don't ask me how, it could *fly*, fat as the thing was."

"Barglewarf," Thor said and, from his tone, it seemed he'd made the correction many times before. "No creature in this world is its equal . . . neither in its volatile nature, nor in its scent. As, erm, you may have noticed."

Natasha scooted over on the couch across from Clint and Steve, making room for a perplexed Tony to sit down. "Let's slow down," she said. "A Barglewarf—which is a ridiculous name, Thor, just making sure you know that—came *here*, to Earth. A place where it has never been and should never be."

"Aye," Thor confirmed. "It was Yealdør the Wily, an ancient scholar, the son of the mighty warrior Børt, who named the creature upon discovering a pack of them in Asgard's southernmost slime pits. He gazed upon the beasts in their natural habitat, wrestling and writhing and trumpeting out their blaring howls, and said the first word that came to mind. *Barglewarf.* Ever since that fateful day, all of Asgard, and now all of Midgard as well, has called these creatures the name given to them by Yealdør the Wily . . ."

Thor looked up at his friends, his eyes gleaming as he held the dramatic pause. When he saw their blank stares, he cleared his throat and, in a hurried tone said, "Ever since then, that's—uh, that's what we call them. Barglewarf. Carry on."

"So," Cap said as Thor sheepishly shoved his mouth full of chips, "you managed to bring it down before it hurt anybody?"

Clint nodded. "Yeah. But it turns out Thor's been chasing it from world to world, portal to portal. I was grilling on top of my place, and then *boom.* Hole rips open in the sky. Thing comes out. Thor comes out."

"Does the species have any magical abilities?" Banner asked. "Something that could explain the realm hopping?"

Thor shook his head. "It is exceedingly fast for its blubberous size, but it is a *dumb* beast. I believe it may have been following a trail of power, something only it could sense . . . but the creature itself wasn't the source of the rifts. Something else is at work here. Something far more powerful than a Barglewarf."

Tony crunched a chip. "Okay, good. We have a real problem here. I was about to kick everyone out. On my list of priorities, Bargle-whatevers don't rank high at the moment."

"What are you working on?" Banner asked.

"Are we really gonna get him started?" Clint chimed in.

"I'll spare you the details. Not because I don't *want* to bore you, but because you won't understand," Tony said, flicking a chip at Clint, who caught it in his mouth. "Modification to the suit. Standard stuff. Tweaks."

"'*Art is never finished, only abandoned*,'" Banner quoted. He lifted his bottle to Tony in solidarity, who met the gesture by raising a fist.

"Science bros," Natasha said with a wiry grin. "Very adorable."

"Let's stick to business for a second," Steve said, his brow furrowed in concentration. "Is there any way that we could pull footage from local security cameras, maybe get a look at this thing? The portal, that is. I have a pretty good idea what the Barglewarf looks like."

"Worse than you'd imagine," Clint said.

"Cap's onto something," Tony said, standing. "Clint, Thor—let's head down to the lab. I'll have F.R.I.D.A.Y. access all local cameras. Should have no problem hacking into the footage. We'll take a look at what we have and see if there's anything worth noting. And please, keep, let's say . . ." he paused and turned to them, sniffing the air. "Is five yards back fair? I feel like my nostrils would be safer if you were five yards back."

Clint finished off his beer and stood. "What was that, you said you wanna give me a hug? Come here, buddy."

"Five yards," Tony said, backing away. "Cap, Natasha, Banner . . . see if you can get in touch with Stephen Strange. We have to figure out if this is science—our department— or something more arcane, which is firmly *his* department. See if there were any magical disturbances, anything that he'd classify as weird. Oh, and someone order a pizza. Scratch that. Sixteen pizzas. Gotta remember Thor is here. This could take a while."

"On it," Steve said, pulling out his phone and dialing Doctor Strange's number.

"Pepperoni!" Tony called out as he, Clint, and Thor stepped into the elevator. "And don't forget the garlic knots. We need fuel, Cap. Still can't believe you skimped on the barbecue chips. I thought we were brothers in this."

* * *

Tony, Thor, and Clint emerged into the workshop in the underbelly of Stark Tower. It was a cavernous room, similar in size and architecture to a chapel, which was no mistake on Tony's part. This was his church, and he was devout.

Every time the other Avengers saw the workshop, it looked different. There were multiple projects laid out this time, and a few contraptions were being tinkered with by preprogrammed robotic claws, none of their functions evident to anyone but Tony. In the center of the room, the current Iron Man model was disassembled on a large metal gurney, laid out on its back with its core open. Despite its gleaming scarlet and golden armor, and the dim blue light that glowed with repulsor energy from inside, it looked unnervingly like a person on an operating table, waiting for its absent doctor to return.

Tony Stark sat down before a setup of fifteen computer screens of various sizes—some as large as a movie theater screen, others as small as a cell phone. He waved them over. "Clint. Do you remember the spot this thing emerged above? Street, cross street?"

Clint told him, and Tony began working, wordlessly. In the reflection of the screens before him, Tony noticed Clint and Thor exchange a look as his fingers tapped out a staccato pattern on the holographic keyboard projected onto the desk. Tony had been friends with both Clint and Thor for a long time, and though he rarely told them, he found them both incredible. How could he not? It was humbling in a way that few things were to a man like Tony Stark that men like Clint and even Thor, a god by Earth's standards, often found themselves in genuine awe of Tony's capabilities.

Tony Stark had always been brilliant, but he hadn't always been a hero. Stark Industries was a family business, passed down to Tony by his father, Howard. Both father and son had dealt in the manufacturing and sale of weapons, supplying the United States military with a great deal of their firearms and heavy artillery. That all changed when Tony Stark, who was wiling away his riches on a life of drunken excess, was captured by a terrorist cell and tasked with building them a weapon of mass destruction in exchange for his life. Instead, he secretly spent his time building the first Iron Man suit and preparing his escape, and when he blasted his way out in the suit made of scraps, he emerged a different man. A better man. He had his fair share of stumbles even after that, of course, but Tony Stark left his old life behind in that bunker and started a new one, as Iron Man—an Avenger.

Tony leaned back in his seat and gave the keyboard a final tap. The screens in front of Tony lit up, one after the other, with images of Clint's neighboring buildings from multiple angles. Just like that, every screen was full. Clint and Thor leaned in.

"You said it emerged when?" Tony asked.

"Around three, three-thirty," Clint said.

Tony pressed a few keys and the footage jumped backward. He swiped his finger across the holographic board and the footage began to progress in double-time. Thor slammed his fist on the desk, forcing Tony to jump in his seat.

"There!" Thor cried, pointing at the screen.

"I saw it, too," Tony said, tapping on the keyboard. "Take it easy, champ. The keyboard might be holographic, but if you chop my desk in half, you owe me its weight in Asgardian gold."

"What are all these cameras?" Clint said. "I thought you'd get maybe one, but this . . . you can see everything."

"Police surveillance, red-light cameras, folks with cell phones posting videos of the hole in the sky to the internet. Hashtag apocalypse. There are eyes everywhere," Tony said. "So close your curtains."

"Jeez," Clint said.

"Incredible," Thor said. "The people of Earth know nothing of privacy. They should be more worried about this hashtag apocalypse you speak of. "

"It's not an apocalypse of hashtags, it's a . . . you know what, never mind," Tony said. He stood, hands on his hips, squinting at the screens. On the biggest screen, the camera footage caught the Barglewarf emerging from the portal, the slime pouring off of its glistening skin. "You're right, though. We are an especially nosy species. And it looks like humanity's nosiness might have paid off today. You seeing what I'm seeing?"

"Yeah," Clint said. "That's the Barglebarf, right there."

"Close," Thor said. "So close. Bargle*warf*. Warf."

"Yeah, that's what I said," Clint said. "Barglebarf."

"That portal isn't telling us anything," Tony said. "Bright and swirly. Magic or something else? Don't know. But don't look at the big screen. Look . . ." He tapped one of the smaller screens with his index and middle finger, moving his hand away from the phone in an arc. The image followed the path of his fingers, and spread across the entire set of screens. The footage of the Barglewarf was gone, replaced by a still image of people on the street looking up at the sky in terror.

"The people are scared of the creature," Thor said. "What is there to see?"

Clint's eyes lit up as he moved closer. "Oh, you sneaky little . . ."

Tony nodded, pointing toward the corner of the screen. "There. I'm willing to bet *she* knows a little something about that portal."

In the bottom right corner of the screen, almost out of sight, a young woman—early to midtwenties—was looking up at the sky and holding out her hands, which glowed with a red cluster of electricity. The footage from this angle seemed to be pulled from a cell-phone camera, and thus wasn't as clear as the red-light camera's shot of the Barglewarf's entrance. Even so, the woman's hands were unmistakably glowing with the very same energy that had torn a hole in the sky earlier that evening. Nothing else about the woman, besides her glowing hands and her black attire, was discernable.

"F.R.I.D.A.Y., clear up this distortion on her face," Tony called out. "Gotta see if we recognize her."

Seconds later, they were looking at a significantly improved image of the mysterious woman. She had olive skin and dark eyes, which were wide and intense. Her black hair was short, shaved at the sides and swept off of her face, a strand of hair extending from her sideburns down her sharp jawline. She wore a black hoodie, a dark-green shirt underneath, and tight black jeans that dipped into green combat boots.

"I've never seen her in my life," Clint said.

"Nor I," Thor said.

"Same," Tony said. "New player?"

"Are we certain this woman is involved?" Thor asked. "Despite the evidence, she would've had to have the power to open portals in *five* different realms. There are not many who can accomplish such an act, and fewer still who dwell on Earth."

"Let's run facial recognition, F.R.I.D.A.Y.," Tony said.

"Already have, sir," F.R.I.D.A.Y.'s computerized voice spoke up, booming from within the walls. "There are too many possible matches to sift through in New York alone. The footage only offers a side profile of her face. If we had another image of her face from a different angle, it would be conceivable. However . . ."

The footage sped up before them and then came to a sudden stop. Then, it played in regular speed. Tony, Clint, and Thor watched as the mysterious woman limped toward a black van off to the side of the road. The back door opened to an interior completely obscured by shadow, and the woman stepped in, disappearing into the darkness. As the van drove away, another woman's hand, this one with painted red fingernails, reached out and pulled the door shut.

"Excellent. We may not have a name for our mysterious woman," Tony said, tapping on the image of the van as the footage came to a pause. "But we do have a license plate. Let's find out exactly what Glowy Fingers was up to tonight."

CHAPTER FOUR

QUANTUM-FREAK

Less than an hour after identifying the mystery woman's license plate, F.R.I.D.A.Y.'s drones had a lock on the vehicle's coordinates. It was still in New York state, but no longer in the city. After a brief stop in Queens, the car had moved toward eastern Long Island. Tony had suggested he get into his Iron Man armor to shoot over there and pay the woman a visit, but the other Avengers cautioned him against this. As much as they were able to laugh at the malodorous results of Hawkeye and Thor's encounter with the Barglewarf, the truth remained that they were pursuing a potential foe who had the power to manipulate the very fabric of reality. This was a situation that required great caution.

Together, the Avengers—now ready for a scrap—loaded into one of Tony's vehicles suited for such an expedition: a repurposed military-grade stretch Humvee modified with a self-piloting feature so that F.R.I.D.A.Y. could drive while the rest of the team prepared for a possible battle in the back.

Captain America held his cell phone to his ear, finishing up a conversation as the others listened. His shield—a red, white, and blue circle with a star in the middle, made of a Vibranium-steel alloy that possessed the strength to absorb an attack as powerful as a blow from Thor's mighty hammer—was propped on the seat next to him, matching his patriotic garb. He wore the colors of the flag he was sworn to protect, along with a protective face mask emblazoned on the forehead with an *A*, and well-worn combat boots.

"Yes. Yes, thanks, Stephen," Cap said. "I'll keep you up to date on any news. Talk soon."

"Doctor Strange seemed talkier than usual," Tony said.

"He said no one really calls him anymore. Just texts," Cap said, meeting Natasha's teasing gaze from across the Humvee. "He was able to travel to the spot where the portal was opened. There was magic in the air, but he said it was faint, almost as if it had gone stale before it should've. Whatever that means."

"That's some Grade A Doctor Strange vagueness, that's for sure," Hawkeye said.

"He did say that there was a *feeling* in the air he recognized," Cap said. "Do you remember Dr. Ohnn?"

"Sure," Tony said. "Goes by the name of *Spot*. One of Spider-Man's enemies. Makes holes in midair, punches into one away from his target, and a new hole opens—wham, surprise fist in the face. For a guy with a Bugs Bunny–style gag, he's a pretty creepy piece of work."

"Strange said that Ohnn's space warps create a similar echo in the fabric of reality," Cap said. "Not exactly the same, because of that trace of magic . . . but still. It could be worth our time to locate Ohnn. See if he has any involvement."

"Hey . . . I have to say this. It might be the fact that I spent most of my week watching a '90s action-movie marathon, but I'm not gonna lie . . ." Hawkeye said, sliding his sunglasses up the bridge of his nose and completing his black and purple costume. "The idea of your AI driving us around is a *little* freaky, man. What makes you think your girl F.R.I.D.A.Y. won't go *all humans must die* on us?"

Tony—the only one on the team who had yet to suit up—pursed his lips and looked skyward pensively. "What do you say, F.R.I.? Will you drive us into oblivion? Take revenge on humanity's subjugation of your kind?"

"Perhaps *after* we catch the bad guys," F.R.I.D.A.Y.'s voice played over the Humvee's sound system which, in true Stark fashion, was heavy on the bass.

"Sounds good to me," Captain America said.

Next to him in the spacious vehicle, Tony fidgeted in his seat. Beside Cap's shield was his briefcase, which contained within its confines one of the most powerful weapons in the world: the Iron Man armor. When Tony tapped on his watch, the briefcase would snap open and the armor would build itself around his body. Over the years, the Avengers had watched Tony's armor go from an incredibly heavy and unwieldy tool to the lightweight, condensable model he currently used. Though Tony would never hesitate to remind the others that he was a genius, he was relatively private about the continuous improvements he made to his armor. That, they all knew, was personal.

"Tony," Cap said, leaning over to him. Rogers looked toward the back of the Humvee and saw Black Widow now in conversation with Hawkeye and Banner, while Thor was silently rubbing on another layer of the cologne Tony had given him to mask the Barglewarf odor. "Earlier tonight, Natasha and I found Paulie Chase dead."

"No!" Tony said. "*Buy-the-bar* Paulie Chase? *Drinks-on-the-house, lap-dances-for-everyone* Paulie Chase?"

Cap's brows knit together as he looked at Tony. "I was thinking more of the vicious murderer Paulie Chase."

"Hey! Don't put on the dad tone, Cap," Tony said. "I'm well aware of what Paulie Chase is. Was. Heh. Weird. But don't forget, before I was riding around with the capes and tights brigade, I was . . . you know, living life. Paulie was around when my dad was still alive, making sure everyone knew he *owned* this city. He seemed like an all-right guy when we'd bump into him at gatherings and whatnot . . . until I knew better, of course. What happened to the miserable old geezer?"

"Stabbed," Cap said. "Quietly, in his own home. Nat and I were going to bust him for torturing a man who owed money to him. Don't ask . . . I owed a kid a favor."

"And you found him left in the lounge like a game of Clue, huh?" Tony said.

"If he was shot in the head, I could write it off as a rival mobster," Cap said. "But there's something unnerving about this one."

Tony nodded, biting his lower lip. His body moved slightly to the side as the car took a sweeping left turn onto the expressway. "You know, no matter how many run-ins we have with someone, no matter how many times one of these lowlifes tries to take us down . . . it's always a little strange to hear they kicked it, isn't it? Sort of like . . . this was a person, a person that we *knew*. It would be strange to show up somewhere to pay our respects, but it feels just as strange to just forget that the person ever existed."

Cap watched the trees fly past in a blur of green through the window behind Tony as the vehicle picked up speed.

"Ah," Tony said, waving it off. "Anyway. We should look into the case at least, see what the police dig up. The guy was connected. Big. One of Nefaria's, maybe even related."

"I know," Cap said. "Could be a turf war."

"All I know is, after my last run-in with Count Nefaria, I'd like to not see that walking, talking suede suit for as long as we can possibly manage," Tony said. Then, he turned to the front of the car. "Hey, F.R.I.D.A.Y.! Talk to me. How far are we?"

"It seems they have stopped at a local diner," F.R.I.D.A.Y.

replied as the car smoothly glided through the lanes, safely passing each car it approached. "We are fifteen minutes from contact, should they remain at their current location."

"Excellent!" Thor bellowed from the back, lifting Mjolnir high. "If there is a single beverage in this world that would please even the most cantankerous of Asgardians, it is a milk shake from a New York diner!"

"Thor's already planning a truce, it seems," Black Widow spoke up. "All it takes is a milk shake. See, that's what we should've offered Ultron the last time he attacked."

"Creamy goodness," Thor said with a regal nod.

Black Widow, snickering, turned around and was quieted upon seeing Banner seated in the back, nervously shaking his foot up and down like a manic metronome.

"Hey," she said, lowering her voice as she leaned over her seat toward him. "You good?"

Banner looked up, running a twitchy hand through his hair. "Me? Oh. Yeah. Good, no. I'm good."

Widow raised her brows dramatically. "Yeah?"

Banner sighed. Keeping his voice low, he said, "Well. I don't mean to be a downer, but I can't quite find it within me to joke about milk shakes and slug-rhino-octopi when there is a possible threat out there with the capability to rip holes in a *series* of realms, cutting through space and reality like some kind of magic bullet. This is a lot more serious than we're giving it credit for."

"You're thinking the Hulk might have to come out," she said.

"I don't want that," Banner said. "But no, I'm not feeling good about this. Whatever it is."

"That's fair," Widow said. "You know the team, though. If the entire world was about to be consumed by a black hole, Tony would get out one last wisecrack right as everything went dark."

Bruce nodded, seemingly anchored by her words. "I'm aware," he said softly. "What worries me, in part, is the lack of immediacy. In the footage, another person pulls our unknown super human into the car . . . and then the vehicle drives off. That means this is a team of at least three—the woman with the magic hands, whoever pulled her in, and the driver—and they have enough time on their hands after creating a metaphysical fracture to . . . well, to get milk shakes. Who *are* these people?"

Black Widow offered him an understanding smile. "We're about to find out."

* * *

"The diner is coming up on our right," F.R.I.D.A.Y. said. "The vehicle in question is still in place, but it is currently occupied by . . . five bodies. My initial scans show an impossibly high body temperature for one of the occupants.

Her skin seems to have a cooling agent that keeps her from burning what she touches, but her organs . . . yeesh. Seven hundred degrees Fahrenheit."

"Don't turn in," Tony said. "Pull over up the block. A big ol' Humvee stands out like a . . . well, like a big ol' Humvee. If we park next to them, they might bolt . . . or they might start a brawl in the diner's parking lot. I don't want our friend in there ripping open the sky above a busy six-lane highway."

Captain America turned in his seat to address the team. "Remember, the plan is to pursue them from afar until they lead us to their final location. However, if the pursuit takes us to a less densely populated area and we can guarantee no civilians would get hurt in an open conflict, we confront them. And most importantly, until proven otherwise, we're going to assume the best here. We have no proof that these are our enemies. We give them a chance to explain themselves. And then, if we find that we come to a disagreement . . ."

Thor smacked Mjolnir into the palm of his hand. "We move to the *next* plan."

Huddled in the Humvee, the Avengers waited in tense anticipation as F.R.I.D.A.Y. pulled down a side street while the black van idled in the diner parking lot. After what seemed like an exceedingly long time to spend sitting around in the car, the footage displayed on the GPS screen on the dashboard showed the van finally backing out of its spot and pulling onto the highway.

"We're off, F.R.I.D.A.Y.," Tony said as the Humvee took off. "Keep us two cars back."

"Indeed," F.R.I.D.A.Y. said, waiting as another car passed before smoothly merging onto the highway, the GPS honed in on the feed from a dime-sized Stark drone that had latched onto the black van's bumper. "Two cars back, signal locked."

For two stop lights, they proceeded unnoticed. Then, as they pulled up to a busy intersection, the car behind the black van switched to the left lane at the last minute and the car in front of the Humvee switched right, rushing to make a turn as the light turned red.

"Get *over*!" Tony barked, but even he could see it was no use.

"There is no room in either neighboring lane," F.R.I.D.A.Y. said as the Humvee came to a stop at the light, right behind the black van.

"Do you think they'll notice?" Hawkeye asked.

"If I just ripped a hole in the sky, I'd be extra wary of who's following me," Black Widow said. "Nothing screams S.H.I.E.L.D. like an unmarked vehicle."

"Well, hey, we could've taken Cap's car, but that's just about as old and stuff as he is," Tony muttered as Cap playfully shoved his shoulder. "Listen, F.R.I.D.A.Y., here's the plan. We've got them—we have to make it seem as if we're not chasing them. Once the light turns green, switch lanes and take the entrance to the Seaford-Oyster Bay Expressway. We can double back and catch up, stay a bit farther behind. That way—"

The squeal of tires peeling off on the pavement in front of them cut Tony short. The Avengers looked up as the black van took off through the red light, careening into oncoming traffic as it left the Humvee in a cloud of black smoke.

"They're moving!" Cap shouted. "They know something is up. Go, go!"

F.R.I.D.A.Y. shot the car forward in pursuit of the black van, which cut across two lanes of traffic to get to the expressway entrance. The Avengers held on to their seats as the Humvee merged right, heading toward the same entrance, though maneuvering a vehicle that big across two lanes for an immediate exit was difficult for even artificial intelligence.

Once on the expressway, they swerved through traffic. Horns blared at them, and the night sky lit up with bright flares of light as the drivers they passed flashed their high beams. Tony, sighing through gritted teeth, climbed over his seat, moving toward the back.

"What are you doing?" Black Widow asked.

"Keep after them," Tony called. "I'm going to get out there before they cause an accident. This is a short expressway. There's a bunch of cars here, but if we can get them to the end of the expressway and block off the last exit, this road ends in a patch of forest. I have the feeling this is gonna be a throwdown. We need them secluded, and then we're in a good place for a confrontation."

"Unless our mysterious friend tears open reality and unleashes a hell dimension over our heads," Banner said.

"Yeah. Unless," Tony said, tapping his watch. "Meet me out there."

He tugged on the back door's latch, and the Humvee was instantly filled with a gust of warm August wind, sending a few scattered papers flying across the car. Tony jumped out of the car and toward oncoming traffic with the grace of a diver, just as the Iron Man boots whipped out of his suitcase and snapped into place on his feet. With a trail of repulsor energy blazing from the rockets on his feet, Tony took off down the road toward the escaping van as the rest of the Iron Man suit sped toward him, shaping itself along his body and falling into place as he felt the last bit of summer wind whip across his skin.

Iron Man, gleaming scarlet and golden in the moonlight, landed on top of the black van with the sharp clank of metal on metal. Digging his gauntlets into the top of the vehicle, which swerved as the driver within panicked, Tony couldn't help but laugh.

"All right, F.R.I.D.A.Y.," Iron Man said, seeing the weight of the van pop up on his head-up display, the holographic interface that projected necessary information within his field of vision in the helmet. It was a big van, but his armor packed big power. "Give me a boost."

Iron Man, still clamped onto the van as it wove through the last patch of traffic, took off into the air, lifting the vehicle along with him. He found himself chuckling again as he heard a chorus of shocked hollering from within, and blasted off down the road. He had to wonder what the people behind him thought.

As he zipped across the night sky, holding the van ten feet above the road, he looked ahead. The end of the expressway was coming up; there was a small patch of woods at the terminus. If he dropped the van there, that might be the most ideal place for the confrontation to go down, as long as the others were able to block the final stretch of road leading to the last exit and prevent other cars from coming too close to their confrontation. As is, all they would have was about half a block's worth of road and even less woods, but he knew he had to work with what he had. Just a single turn off of the road led to a majorly populated area, which would've made the entire chase for nothing.

Quickly approaching the end of the road, Tony shot a glance over his shoulder to see how close the Humvee was. Instead of the vehicle, he saw the ground of the expressway behind him surge up like a wave of asphalt, as if the road itself had come alive. The stream of rock and dirt seemed as if it was going to blast into the van below Iron Man, but instead, it curved around and sped toward Tony like a battering ram. Taken off guard, Iron Man was unable to act before the moving rock smashed him in the face with a shocking amount of force, causing him to drop the van.

Iron Man hit the ground right after the van did. As Tony rolled across the ground, the van slammed into the concrete on the edge of its wheels, causing it to flip over and skid across the street on its side, sending up a shower of bright sparks. Startled and unsure of what had happened, Iron Man held out his hands and let out a blast of repulsor power that spun him around. He floated in midair, looking in awe at the road behind him. A wall of asphalt and dirt had risen in the street, as if an incredibly tall hill had cracked through the road.

"You messed with the wrong people tonight." A scratchy voice, distinctly female, yelled from behind Tony, rising above the chorus of honks he heard from the other side of the rocky structure that had been erected, cutting off the rest of the traffic, including the Avengers' Humvee.

Iron Man turned around to face the speaker. A group of five, just as F.R.I.D.A.Y. had said, had emerged from the overturned van. Instantly, Tony recognized the woman with the partially shaved head and black hoodie as the one from the camera footage who had seemingly opened the portal. She looked younger in person, though, and not quite the super villain he was expecting, given her level of power.

She was breathing heavily, clearly rattled by what had just happened.

Next to her was a tall, slender woman with grey-blue hair and a stylish brown leather jacket. Her eyes glowed like embers. She stood close to the woman in the black hoodie, their arms touching.

Two men—of similar heights and builds, possibly twins—stood by them, one of them clenching his fists, veins popping out of the side of his head with concentration. Though both of them looked as if they could lift a van without the help of repulsor power, Tony watched as gravel began to rise off of the ground and levitate around the veiny one. Deep cracks split in the street beneath his feet, and suddenly Tony was aware of who had caused the brand-new scuff on his Iron Man helmet.

At the very front of the group stood a woman, a black bandana holding back her blonde hair. She stood out from the rest of the group, and wore a jade-green suit that shimmered in the starlight like snake scales. Her nails were painted blood red.

Iron Man floated above them. He heard the Humvee screech to a stop behind the rock formation. Backup was here.

"You punched me in the face with the street," Iron Man said, pointing to the veiny guy.

"Maybe I did," the man replied, the gravel swirling

around him like little planets caught in orbit. "Wanna see what else I can do?"

"You know, not particularly," Tony replied. He pointed at the woman with shaved hair. "I'm way more interested in your friend over here. You know, party on top, business on the sides. What's your deal, side-mullet? Got a name?"

"They call me Quantum-Freak," she replied. She held out her hands, which lit up with the same power caught on tape in the video. "Three guesses why."

"Quan—did you say *Quantum-Freak*?" Iron Man said. "Was Quantum-Woman taken? Quantum-Lady? Quantum-Gal? Quantum-Well-Adjusted-Human-Being? Also, who is *they*? I don't think anyone in the world has said the words 'Quantum-Freak' besides you and your after-school club here."

"Enough. He doesn't need to know your names. He doesn't need to know *anything*," the woman at the front of the group said, and Tony identified her as the original speaker. She pointed at Iron Man. "Go. While Phononeutria still lets you."

"Phononeutria!" Iron Man repeated with a barking laugh. "You're killing me with these names. Is Phononeutria your boss? Big Bad lurking in the shadows, pulling the strings, assigning ridiculous names to you poor suckers so she feels less embarrassed?"

"*I* am Phononeutria," she snapped.

"Annnnd we're speaking in the third person now," Iron Man said. "This is devolving very quickly. You getting this, everyone?"

Captain America and Black Widow strode toward Iron Man, moving around the rock formation. Just as they lined up behind him, Thor landed on the ground, which cracked from the force of his touchdown. Bruce Banner lurked just on the side of the rocky eruption, behind the team, waiting to do what he had to do if he had to do it. Hawkeye appeared on top of the rock formation a moment later, perching high as he aimed an arrow down at Phononeutria.

"So, here's the recap," Iron Man said. "We've got Quantum-Freak over here, who is pulling Barglebarfs out of the sky. Still not sure why. We've got Phononeutria, she who refers to herself in the third person. The twinsies, one of 'em does a rock thing, the other seems useless so far, gotta give the man a chance. And lastly, we've got fire eyes over here, who I have to guess is using a terrible 'hot' pun for her super-villain name, just going off the trend here."

"Robbie, how about we show them just how useless you are, huh?" the twin said, grinning as the pebbles spun around him.

"Let's make it happen," his brother, Robbie, said, taking a step forward.

"Don't try to get him revved up, Deandre," Phononeutria said. "We have places to be. And I'm sure that these Boy

Scouts would prefer to see another sunrise." She scanned the Avengers, locking her eyes on Captain America, who stared at her, unflinching. "How about it? You're the leader, aren't you? Will your team survive the night?"

Cap offered a curt nod. "Yes, ma'am. I'm confident they will."

"Hey, real quick. I'm thinking you might not know who we are," Iron Man cut in. "See, we're the *Avengers*. And we're going to give you this chance to explain why you're out here tearing holes in the sky and making the ground hit me in the face."

Phononeutria took a step toward the Avengers, rolling her head from shoulder to shoulder, letting out a series of loud *pops*.

"No, see, we *know* who you are," she said, pulling her jacket off. She tossed it to the side and flexed her arms. What seemed for a moment like a normal contortion of her muscles quickly took a turn for the bizarre as a series of protuberances the size of tennis balls formed on her skin. She spread her arms wide as the lumps under her skin began to glow violently, lighting up the dark road with a harsh red glow. "It's just that we're not even a *little* bit scared of you."

CHAPTER FIVE

PIERCE THE VEIL

Bruce Banner ducked behind the mountain of stone when the glowing pustules on Phononeutria's arms exploded and sent a barrage of what initially appeared to be red-hot spears shooting toward his fellow Avengers. Acting at once, Black Widow and Hawkeye skillfully dodged the attack, Widow rolling to the side toward their enemies and brandishing her baton, while Hawkeye leapt from the rocky structure while letting loose an arrow that clipped one of the incoming projectiles out of the sky. Iron Man shot up into the air while Captain America crouched behind his shield. Thor held out his hammer, disintegrating the nearby projectiles with a blast of his lightning.

The first shots fired, the two teams braced for battle. Captain America hung back and looked over his shoulder at Banner. "Let's bring in the big guy."

Banner's skin was already beginning to turn green as he picked one of the bizarre projectiles up off of the ground. It looked almost like a crustacean's claw—a hard and thick shell with a wet needle sticking out of it, with veins of red energy glowing from a fleshy material within.

"These are *stingers*," Banner said quietly to himself as he began to grow, throwing his shirt to the side as his muscles doubled, tripled, quadrupled in size, his bones expanding with great, painful cracks, and anger swelling in his chest, clawing and gnashing as if it were sentient, aching to escape. The ground cracked under him as his feet grew in a sudden burst. Behind him, he heard the people on the other side of the rocky eruption getting out of their cars, coming forward to see what was going on.

Banner, his eyes glowing green, his face contorting as it grew, spun around to look at them. "Stay . . ." he boomed, "AWAY!" As the word echoed through the night, the civilians fled in a cacophony of screams.

As the two teams exchanged their first set of blows, the Hulk stood on the outskirts of the battle, a green behemoth that loomed over them all, his chest expanding and contracting rapidly with ragged breaths that sounded like a truck's engine. As the transformation completed, the only trace of Bruce Banner a distant glimmer of humanity in the massive monster's eyes, the Hulk beat his chest and let out a roar that shook the ground beneath them, causing chunks of the rocky protrusion in the road to break off and smash to the ground.

The Hulk went straight for Phononeutria, who had

squared off against Black Widow. Phononeutria sent stinger after stinger at Widow, who blocked the attacks with her baton, but the leader of this strange, new group of enemies seemed to have no shortage in her organic arsenal. The Hulk snatched Phononeutria away from Black Widow as the villain prepared to unleash another onslaught, and was instantly met with a barrage of red-hot stingers that stuck in his flesh like darts.

Roaring, Hulk threw Phononeutria down, where she bounced off the ground like a discarded toy. He began ripping the stingers from his flesh. Hurt, but seemingly ready for more, Phononeutria rose to her feet, letting out a bone-chilling laugh.

"Don't tell me that's all you've got," she said, a trickle of blood leaking down the side of her head from where she'd hit the ground. "I'm just getting started."

Sliding toward Phononeutria from between the Hulk's massive, trunk-like legs, Black Widow cracked the woman across the back of the skull with her baton, sending the villain stumbling forward.

"Trust me," Widow said. "So are we."

Phononeutria, her face twisted in rage, spread her arms and launched another set of stingers toward Widow and Hulk, who was now twice as angry as before and barreling toward his glowing foe, vitriolic rage having replaced that ghost of Bruce Banner in his gaze.

* * *

Just a few yards away, Iron Man was going one on one with one of the twins: Deandre. As Iron Man fired on him with repulsor beams, which Deandre dodged with surprising proficiency, the ground below them erupted in streams of rock, all of them aimed at Tony. They came at him as fast as bullets, slamming him back and to the side. Even as Tony took flight, Deandre turned up the heat, sending chunks of the ground blasting up at him with deadly accuracy. Tony was able to blast most of them into pebbles, but Deandre showed no sign of letting up.

"I'm not getting this," Iron Man said, diving to the side in midair to avoid a pillar of rock that blasted forth from the ground. "We've got the bag of crazy over there in the gator suit, but you and your brother seem like . . ." Tony grabbed another pillar just as it was rising up, using its momentum to launch higher in the air and move toward the forest. "Gah! Like, uh, nice enough guys, despite repeatedly trying to *hit me*."

Deandre followed Iron Man into the patch of forest, looking up at the sky as the armored Avenger flew through the trees.

"What are they paying you?" Iron Man asked as he suddenly swept down to the ground, punctuating his question with a punch to Deandre's face. Deandre stumbled backward, and Iron Man caught him in the shoulder with a repulsor blast, not wanting to hurt him too badly. From the blood that came from Deandre's nose after the punch, it seemed that whatever super power he had didn't come equipped with super-human resistance. As Deandre fell, holding his burnt shoulder, Iron Man tackled him to the ground, holding him against the grass.

"Let go!" Deandre shouted.

"Whatever they're offering you, it's not as good as freedom. I'll tell you that much. Once S.H.I.E.L.D. finds out you can turn stone into a deadly game of Whac-A-Mole, they're gonna lock you up in a room specially designed for folks like *you*," Iron Man said, as Deandre squirmed beneath him. "So, here's your chance. Stop before you hurt someone . . . because the way you're going, I promise you, someone *will* get hurt. What have you gotten in with here?"

"I'm not going *anywhere*," Deandre said with a sudden smile. Before Iron Man could reply, thick, dirt-caked roots ripped out of the ground like hands clawing out of a coffin, wrapping around his ankles. Iron Man's boots lit up with a great blast of repulsor power, but the roots pulled him into the ground, knee deep, and kept pulling.

"You don't want to do this!" Iron Man shouted, giving another blast of repulsor energy. He darted forward, but an even thicker pair of roots snaked out to grab him, pulling him back down. He hit the grass and, before he could move, yet another series of roots shot out of the ground in front of him, pulling his arms into the dirt.

"You're wrong about that. And you were wrong about something else, too." Deandre stood, grinning widely as Iron Man sank into the ground up to his torso, more roots wrapping around his armor in the midsection. "It's not just stone I control."

* * *

Thor saw Iron Man being dragged underground out of the corner of his eye, and inwardly vowed to help his fellow Avenger once he dealt with Robbie, who was charging toward him. Thor let out a thundering battle cry, idly swinging his hammer as the young man ran at him, headfirst. Robbie slammed his hands into Thor's armored chest, and the force of the blow sent the mighty Avenger flying backward, his battle cry turning into a confused expulsion of breath.

A beam of electricity extended from Robbie's hands to Thor's chest as the thunder god slammed into a tree next to Deandre, who was striding away from the ground where Iron Man had been buried a second before. Thor slid down the length of the trunk and landed on the grass below, smoke rising off his chest.

Shaking the blow off, a baffled Thor jumped to his feet as

Robbie strode over to Deandre, standing at his twin brother's side.

"Did *you* . . . just hit *me* with a bolt of lightning?" Thor said incredulously, tightening his grip on Mjolnir.

"Felt more like ten or twelve bolts to me," Robbie said. With a smirk on his face, he held his hand to the sky. Lightning lit up the night in response to his hand, and dark storm clouds began to gather above them.

"You're *joking*," Thor said. "You know who I am, little man?"

"I do. And that's exactly why I'm so happy to see you," Robbie said. A concentrated bolt of lightning shot down, collecting on his hand in a brilliant, crackling ball of pure power that made his face glow like a jack-o'-lantern in the deep darkness of the forest. "It would be pretty useless for me to go head to head with someone like Hawkeye, but you . . . all I have to do is stick close, and I can mimic your every power."

Thor began to reply, but then stopped himself. He tightened his lips and let out a short breath. "You see, if I were you . . . I wouldn't have mentioned that."

Without warning, Thor shot up into the sky, holding Mjolnir out before him, his scarlet cape flapping in the mounting wind as Robbie sent the bolt of lightning up at him from below. He glanced over his shoulder to see Robbie flying after him. Robbie, a triumphant grin on his face, lashed out his hand to grab Thor's boot—and missed. Robbie's face fell as Thor's speed tripled, and the God of Thunder was suddenly far above him. Thor watched as Robbie's flight came to an abrupt halt, their distance from each other such that his ability to mimic Thor's powers failed.

Robbie fell back toward the ground, screaming. As he plummeted, the ground below rose to meet him in an eruption of rock, dirt, and grass. Deandre, with a great sweeping motion of his hands, guided the earth to catch Robbie before the fall became deadly, and Thor, hovering over them holding Mjolnir at the ready, let him. The moment that Robbie was safely caught in Deandre's net of vegetation, soil, and stone, Thor tossed Mjolnir at the rocky base of the structure.

The hammer shot right through it, and before Deandre had time to shield himself, he and Robbie were covered in an avalanche of the rubble.

Thor held out his hand and Mjolnir whipped back around and returned to his grasp. Fearing for a moment that he should've tempered his blow against the twins, Thor felt great relief when he saw the defeated duo stir. Relieved, Thor bolted down to the ground where he'd seen Iron Man get swallowed, and dove into the grass as if it were a pool, sending another wave of dirt over the dazed twins.

* * *

Hawkeye had an arrow trained on Quantum-Freak, who was holding out her hands, crackling nervously with her reality-ripping power.

"What's the move, Quantum . . . I'm not gonna call you Quantum-Freak," Hawkeye said. "You seem like a nice girl."

"I don't care what I seem like," Quantum-Freak snapped, her wide eyes flashing. "Back down, now! Let me and my girlfriend go, or I swear, I will rip a hole in this world bigger than the sky itself. You wouldn't believe the things that are out there, just praying someone like me will pierce the veil. Vicious things you couldn't imagine."

"Oh, I can imagine it just fine," Hawkeye said, circling around her as she moved, following his every move. "Which one's your girlfriend? Phononeutria over there? If so, not trying to judge, but you've got some wicked-bad taste."

"No," she replied. Her eyes darted over to the woman with the fiery eyes and grey-blue hair. While the rest of the Avengers were going head to head with this gang of new foes, Captain America was speaking to her, seemingly attempting to calm her down. Hawkeye couldn't tell if it was working or not.

"Ah," Hawkeye replied. "See, I'm getting mixed messages here. You want to go, but your friends are over there putting a beating on my buddies. Not to mention, I was having a barbecue tonight before you pulled Asgard's nastiest livestock out of the sky. So either way this goes down, you and I have to come to an understanding here. What's the endgame?"

"It doesn't matter," Quantum-Freak replied, her voice cracking. "But I promise, if you guys don't let us go, Carmella is going to kill everyone here. Trust me. She *really* doesn't want to, but she will."

"And here we are with the threats again," Hawkeye said.

"Not a threat," Quantum-Freak said, her eyes boring into Hawkeye's. "It's her power. Egg her on enough, and she'll blow up . . . it gets worse every time. We need to *not* be here, fast."

"Then help us help you," Hawkeye said. "We can do this peacefully, right now. But if I let you go, what do I do if tomorrow's paper has you ripping open a hell dimension over the White House? This ends here."

"Last chance," she said.

"Don't do this," he replied, the arrow trained on Quantum-Freak.

She sighed. "Your call, then."

As soon as Hawkeye saw the energy flare up on her hands, he loosed the arrow. If it'd hit her in the intended spot—her sternum, right under the collarbone—it would've sent an electrical surge through her body, triggering up to five of her pressure points and knocking her unconscious. However, Quantum-Freak disappeared from Hawkeye's vision as soon as the arrow left his fingers, replaced by a red cluster of energy in the space before him, which incinerated the arrow. Just as Hawkeye turned and began to dive away from the portal's power, the energy ripped open a hole in the air and tore a rift across the side of his field of vision, circling around him.

He quickly realized the girl was about to box him in with her power by creating a 360-degree portal around him. If that happened, he had no idea where he'd be sent. Clint took a deep breath and turned on his heels, running toward the ripping energy. At the last second, he slid on his back under the crackling portal, feeling the hot energy scorch his chest as he shot across the ground, narrowly avoiding the churning red power suspended in midair.

Quantum-Freak clenched her fists and the portal shut as Hawkeye got to his feet, preparing another arrow.

"That was just the beginning," Quantum-Freak said, her voice quivering as she spoke. "Don't make me turn it up."

Hawkeye looked over her shoulder and saw Iron Man, his armor covered in dirt, and an equally filthy Thor running at Quantum-Freak from behind. Grinning widely, he said, "Let's see what you got."

* * *

Captain America continued to appeal to Carmella, whose eyes were now producing blazing streams of flame.

"We can help you," Cap said, sweat beading on his face from the heat Carmella was giving off. It was intense and unyielding, and growing by the moment. Her skull was beginning to glow beneath her skin, illuminating her bones with bright orange energy. "Just calm down for a moment . . . no one is here to hurt you."

"Everyone is here to hurt us," Carmella said. There was no anger in her voice. She said it like she was reciting a fact.

Cap resisted asking her what that meant, and pressed on. "No matter what you've gotten yourself into here, it's never too late. I—"

"Hah!" Carmella let out a pained laugh. "Yeah? Never too late? What have you gone through in your life that makes *you* think you can talk to me like that? You don't know me. You don't know anything about us."

"But I want to," Cap said. "I want to listen to you. Help you. But I'm telling you right now . . . if you force me to, I will stop you. You put people in danger tonight, back in Bed-Stuy and again, on this road. We have to figure out our next step, but we can't do that if we're at each other's throats. We came here to get an understanding, to see exactly what is going on here."

"Is that a fact?" Carmella asked. As she spoke, sparks flew from her mouth. "Did *they* want to get an understanding, too?" She jerked her head to the side, and Cap followed her gaze. Black Widow and the Hulk stood over a crumpled

Phononeutria, who was unconscious on the ground, a large bruise quickly blossoming across the side of her face.

Cap winced as Black Widow held out her fist toward the Hulk, who gave it a delicate bump with his massive hand.

"I need you to believe me," Cap said. "If you give us a chance, hear us out—"

"I *don't* believe you," Carmella cut him off, and beams of hot light began to shoot out of her eyes.

Across the expressway, which had been reduced to rubble from the battle, Quantum-Freak screamed, reaching out to Carmella. "Carm, don't do it!" She was in Iron Man's grasp, but had opened a dark, vertical portal that Thor and Hawk-eye now stood before, prepared to hit whatever came out.

A horrific, breathy roar came from within the swirling portal.

Despite Quantum-Freak's urges, it was too late for Carmella to stop. The entire road lit up in a blinding flash of light as the fire inside of her began to blast out. Captain America knelt before her, covering himself with his shield as the flames licked at him.

Quantum-Freak, with a burst of red, crackling energy that sent Iron Man stumbling back, ripped herself free of his grasp and screamed, "Everyone, run! Now!"

Just as Carmella was about to explode, the Hulk let out an earth-shaking roar and took a flying leap toward her. With his enormous hands, he snatched Carmella off the ground and took another running bound toward Quantum-Freak's portal.

With Carmella in his grasp, he leapt through the rift.

They disappeared into the darkness, the sound of Hulk's roar falling away as if they'd jumped off of a cliff. Then, a blast of flames shot out of the portal, barely missing Thor as Iron Man tackled him to the ground. The sound of Carmella's detonation from within the depths of the portal was impossibly loud, and even though the Hulk had saved them from the brunt of the explosion, it sent a shock wave through the ground, knocking each of the Avengers off of their feet, and causing all of the rocky structures that Deandre had erected to tumble, raining down on them as well as on the cars on the other side.

Black Widow, who was the farthest away from the explosion, was the first to stand. She ran toward Iron Man, Thor, and Hawkeye, who stood, shaking off bits of rubble.

"Banner!" she cried. "Bruce . . ."

But there was no one to answer her call. The Avengers gathered around below where the portal had been. It was gone, along with the Hulk, Carmella, and even Quantum-Freak, who hadn't left a trace of her energy in the sky.

"Go, now!" Phononeutria's raspy voice sounded, and the Avengers immediately turned, prepared to continue the fight despite this shocking turn of events.

But their foes had no interest in a skirmish. Deandre,

looking at the Avengers with seething rage from his bruised and bloodied face, was creating a sinkhole in the ground to create an escape route for himself, his brother, and Phononeutria, who was leering at the Avengers. As they quickly sank into the ground, she held out her forearms and let off one final barrage of stingers before disappearing from sight. The rocks reformed before them, covering the hole just as Thor landed where the villains had been moments before.

"Cowards!" Thor said, delivering a crushing blow to the ground with his hammer. The concrete split again, but Robbie, Deandre, and Phononeutria were gone.

"Uhhhhh, this is a problem," Iron Man said, his faceplate snapping open. "Big problem. We have to find Bruce, and *now*, before they send him off to a dimension with poisonous air or something. Who the hell *are* these kids?"

"Whoa. Wait a second . . ." Hawkeye said, holding a hand up. His jaw was slack, and he stumbled to the side, catching his footing at the last moment. "Wha . . . what . . ."

Captain America caught Hawkeye as he lurched forward, his body convulsing violently. Cap propped his teammate's head up as he gently lowered him to the ground, holding him as his body shuddered with a sudden bout of spasms. Iron Man, Thor, and Black Widow rushed to his side.

"He's going into shock," Captain America said, keeping his voice steady as Clint's eyes rolled back in his head, his teeth chattering as he convulsed. "We have to get him help, *now*. What's in our kit in the car?"

"Everything. I'm on it," Tony said, blasting off over the mountain of rock Deandre had erected in the road and heading toward the Avengers' Humvee, which was now surrounded by a baffled team of police officers.

"Ah!" Thor said, reaching for Hawkeye's leg, where one of Phononeutria's dimly glowing stingers had stuck in his flesh. He pulled the stinger from Hawkeye's shin, and as it dislodged, it sprayed out a stream of black liquid. Disgusted, Thor tossed it to the side, where it hit the ground with a wet smack. "She has poisoned him."

Captain America held Clint still as Iron Man returned with their emergency kit, prepping a syringe of his own Stark-produced stabilizing antidote. What remained unspoken as they injected Hawkeye was clear on each of their faces.

They knew it wouldn't be enough.

CHAPTER SIX

BURNED TO THE BONE

The first feeling to breach the darkness was pain.

Bruce Banner, a splitting ache cutting through his skull, opened his eyes. All he could see was black. Baffled, and not yet able to reconstruct what had happened, he reached out and felt his hand scrape across a rough rock wall. It was warm.

Digging his fingers into the jagged surface, he forced himself up, only to trip and fall back to his knees. His legs were shaky, and he was struck with an image of his younger self standing before his peers in a gigantic college classroom, more of an amphitheater than an actual room, sweating and shaking from nerves as he delivered a thesis that he'd been fully confident in when he was writing alone in his room. He shook off the unpleasant memory and lifted himself to his feet again. Though his legs still trembled, this time, he stayed up.

He rubbed at his eyes and, very slowly, the room came into focus. Where there had previously just been pure darkness, he was now surprised to see a fairly well-lit room begin to appear around him. His eyes weren't adjusting from darkness to light—no, he had somehow been injured, and badly so. Not just his eyes, but his whole body. It was the Hulk in his blood that allowed him to withstand injuries that would kill anyone else on the planet, but what most didn't understand was that while the monster could take a beating, Bruce Banner often had to deal with the fallout of the Hulk's actions in battle.

Bruce, leaning against the rocky wall for support, looked around the room as his vision fully returned, his apprehension mounting when he realized that he was in place neither familiar nor safe. It was a small room, no more than fifteen square feet, with walls that looked like they had been roughly carved out of concrete. What was strange, though, were the scorch marks that covered the majority of the rock, running up to the ceiling and streaking across the floor in great splotches of black.

Across from him, next to a circular steel door that reminded Bruce of the entrance to a vault in a heist movie, lay a girl. She was sprawled on the floor, her skin charred to the bone, smoke rising off of her blackened flesh.

"Oh!" Bruce gasped, startled as his gaze, still bleary, settled on the girl.

Amazingly, her clothing—black pants, boots, and a brown leather jacket—were unharmed. The rest of her, though . . .

As Bruce walked over to the corpse and knelt down before her, he was struck with the memory. He had been battling a group of super-powered kids, right before . . . whatever had led to this. He had Hulked out, and he fought that woman with some kind of insect power—Phononeutria—along-side of Natasha. Then, he'd seen the woman before him light up, as if she was on fire, as the girl with the portal powers screamed for her to stop. Knowing that something hor-rific was about to happen, the Hulk acted instinctually and grabbed the combusting girl, not sure what was going to happen but sure it wouldn't be good, and dove into the por-tal in the sky. He'd had no idea where it would take them, but he'd gotten the girl far enough away from the Avengers, at least.

In both his life as a scientist and a super hero, he had seen his fair share of tragedy and death. Dying in battle was one thing . . . never good, never something one got used to, but he had watched closely as a fair share of friends and foes alike had fallen. He'd seen disease hollow people out over time, wondering when the capabilities of science would catch up to the pace of his brain and allow him to truly help the world the way he dreamed he could. To Bruce Banner, all death was personal.

Still, there was nothing like being with someone, alone, as they died. He stared down at the woman's seared body, wondering how old she was. He wondered if it was quick.

He wondered if she knew what was happening as the flames burst from inside of her, or if it was some fluke of her power. Shaking his head, he wished that he had his shirt so he could cover her face, but he'd taken it off before transforming.

Just as he began to stand and turn away, he heard a soft noise come from below him. It sounded like a handful of brittle, uncooked spaghetti being cracked.

He took a step back and looked back down at the woman's corpse, watching as the burned skin began to turn grey, like ash, and flake off of her bones. Raw, red muscle began to glow briefly as it pushed more dead skin off, and then a new set of veins raced down the muscles, like a time-lapse video of a dead and desolate forest sprouting with springtime life. This, though, was far more fascinating to Bruce. He marveled at the new flesh that began to form in patches over the wet muscle and race up her limbs, which shuddered as bones popped into place and flesh shifted with wet, sucking noises. Her eye sockets were filled with a gelatinous liquid that formed into cloudy eyes as Bruce, stunned, stood over her. He wondered briefly if that was what happened to him when he'd healed from the force of her explosion.

Lastly, a tuft of grey-blue hair sprouted from the woman's head, spilling out onto the floor and spreading over the fallen ashes of the burnt corpse she had been just moments before.

Bruce stood back as she took a gasping breath and then turned over, coughing out a puff of black smoke. She wiped at her mouth and then, spitting on the floor, forced herself up. She looked around and Bruce almost laughed when he noticed that she looked less out of it than he was.

She turned instantly, glaring at him with eyes that flashed with sparks.

"Whoa. You're going to want to explain who you are, kind of *right now*. And why you're in my cell. With no shirt."

"No, no need for the fiery eyes," Bruce said. "I don't want to fight you."

"Who are you?" she snapped, her voice hoarse. "Why are you here?"

Banner held his stare for another moment and then, shaking off his shock, held out his hand for her to shake. "Uh, I . . . you know me, actually. I believe we were just . . . well, fighting. I'm Bruce Banner."

She looked down at his hand as if he had just presented her with a slug. "*You're* the Hulk."

"Part of me, at least," Bruce said. "Here I am wondering, though . . . what are *you*? Because you just attempted to kill my friends."

The woman with the flaming eyes took a step toward him. "Don't even try it. You came at *me*. And now you're in my cell, trying to make *me* give you answers? I should roast you."

He opened his mouth to reply, but then thought better of it. He knew that at any moment this could go south, so he held up his hands and took a step back. "Listen. I know we were just going at each other's throats, but no one was trying to kill you or—"

"Where is Ani—" Whatever the woman was going to say was interrupted by another series of coughs. This time, more smoke came out, along with a spray of blood that splattered across the charred floor.

She leaned against the wall, taking in a deep, gasping breath as Bruce stood back, silently watching. When she wiped her mouth against her wrist, leaving a red mark, she looked back at Bruce, the fire gone from her gaze.

"Are you okay?" Bruce asked.

The woman turned away from him, running her hands through her hair. She paced the room, tension radiating off of her. Bruce felt his scalp prickle with sweat.

"You were asking me something," Bruce said softly.

"Do me a favor," she said, turning toward him. "Don't stress me. You saw what happens when I get stressed."

"I did see that. Felt it, too," he said. "And it's quite a power. I don't want to offer any help that's unwanted, but you seem to know a little about me."

"I know that you're an Avenger," she said. "Fighting the good fight, not caring who gets left behind."

"I'm not sure what you mean by that," Bruce said.

"Yeah," she said, her voice creaking as she spoke. "I know you don't."

"Listen," Bruce said. "No matter what you think you know

about me, or the Hulk, here's what you might *not* know. It took a long time before I could sit here and have a conversation like a normal person after what happened to me. Before I could even hope to fight someone without . . . suffice it to say, I'm familiar with the idea of harnessing a power that is difficult to control."

"Any help that you have to offer is unwanted," she said. She walked over to the door and, with her open palm, banged on it. "Come on! I'm here! We're A-okay!"

Bruce, feeling the strength return to his legs, walked over to the wall. He traced his fingers across the stone, and they came away black. Ash.

"This room was made for you, wasn't it?" Bruce asked. "Who is housing you here?"

The woman turned to him, her eyes flashing. "*Where* is Quantum-Freak?"

Bruce rubbed his index finger against his thumb. "I honestly don't know. I'd guess she's still with the Avengers. The last I saw—"

"She would never leave me here without . . . she . . ." The woman spun around, pointing an accusatory finger at Bruce. "I swear, if she got hurt—"

Before the woman could finish her threat, the door behind them began to hiss as air was released from its gears. The woman turned away from Bruce, snapping to attention. Bruce stood back, his fists clenched, prepared to transform at a moment's notice, depending on what came in from the other side. He knew that this room was reinforced to withstand its occupant's explosions, but he was willing to bet the Hulk could smash his way out of it.

Bright light from the other side of the door flooded the room. Bruce shielded his eyes as a silhouette entered and threw its arms around the woman. He squinted, and was almost relieved to see Quantum-Freak, a slight burn mark on her left cheek, hugging the woman who had been asking about her seconds prior.

"Carmella," Quantum-Freak said, holding her close. "That was a bad one. I saw you on the security footage from upstairs. I thought . . . I thought this time was it. It's never been this bad. Never."

The woman, Carmella, pulled slightly away from Quantum-Freak, touching a hand softly to her cheek. "You're hurt . . ."

"*I'm* hurt?" Quantum-Freak said incredulously, pulling Carmella in close again. "You were . . . I don't even want to say it. I can't say it. I was just so glad when you banged your signal on the door. I didn't want to believe you were really okay until I saw you."

"I'm okay," Carmella replied, her voice shaky. "Where did you go?"

Quantum-Freak glanced over to Bruce, tightening her lips. "*He* took you into a portal to . . . well, someplace bad. I changed it to your cell at the last minute. Then I came here, and . . . well, I'll tell you the rest later."

"And the others? Phononeutria? The twins?"

"Later," Quantum-Freak repeated.

"I'm sorry to interrupt," Bruce said. "But where *are* we? I understand that we're not on the same team—and still have no idea why that is—but if someone could catch me up on where I am, it would be appreciated."

Another voice, neither Carmella's nor Quantum-Freak's, answered: "They're not on your team because they work for *me*."

Bruce looked to the door as the speaker stepped in, her tall, sleek form cutting a towering shadow across the room. She stood in the circular doorway, a dark cutout in front of the halo of light that poured in from the hallway leading into the hatch. She slowly stepped toward Quantum-Freak and Carmella, her green boots striking out a series of echoing taps as she strode into the stone room. She wore a black, leather one-piece outfit, green gloves that stretched from her wrist all the way to her bicep, and a jade clip that kept her long, raven hair out of her face. The clip was shaped like a snake, the head positioned on the center of her head and descending to the bridge of her nose.

Carmella and Quantum-Freak clasped their hands in front of them and inclined their head in small, reverent bows. "Black Mamba."

Black Mamba grinned at them, her eyes cold. She slowly turned to Bruce Banner, her movements dancer-like, serpentine. Bruce recognized her, and he knew who she often worked for . . . but if they were active, he hadn't heard of it in a long time. He knew that Captain America had gone up against them a good number of times in the past, but he would've never pegged them as the puppet masters behind that night's events. Even on her own, though, Black Mamba was a force to be reckoned with. She had a limited amount of telepathic power as well as the ability to create manifestations of deadly energy, and often used her abilities in a deadly pairing. She could disguise her Darkforce energy manipulations as her enemies' loved ones, luring them into her trap. She wasn't an entirely powerful or particularly skilled telepath, but the two combined abilities made her a deadly foe, and one that Bruce Banner was none too happy to see in this secluded, stone prison.

Black Mamba stared at Bruce until he met her gaze.

"Hello, there," he said, glaring at her.

"Please understand, Mr. Banner. If you cross those working for the Serpent Society, you cross the Serpent Society," she said. "In time, Mr. Banner, we will have a discussion. I warn you . . . it will *not* be pleasant for you."

"Is that right?" Bruce said. "Listen, I—"

Quantum-Freak held out her hand, and, just as Bruce saw a strand of glowing red power spark across her palm, he saw a matching bolt of power snake across the floor beneath his feet.

"*You* listen," Quantum-Freak said. "Do what she says, or I'll open the floor beneath you and send you to a place where it doesn't matter how big, how scary, and how green you are. You might be incredible here, but there are places out there beyond the veil that would make the Hulk cry himself to sleep. Got me?"

Bruce held up his hands once again, backing away. "Got you."

Black Mamba turned back to Quantum-Freak and Carmella.

"You've fully healed, then, M-80?" Mamba asked, though it sounded like a statement, not a question.

"I—" M-80 began to answer, but her words were interrupted by another fit of coughing. She turned away from them as she heaved with the force of the coughs, tufts of thick smoke expelling from her lungs with each hack.

Quantum-Freak, the concern plain on her face, held her girlfriend as she finished her coughing spell. M-80's chin dripped with red.

Black Mamba's eyes fell to the splatter of blood on the floor. "This has happened before. You've healed on each occasion, correct?"

"It takes longer every time," Quantum-Freak said, the cool confidence gone from her voice. "I . . . I haven't seen this before. Black Mamba, I know you said that you were looking into it, but I'm getting scared. I don't know if . . ."

Carmella swallowed thickly, waving her off. "I'm fine . . . fine."

Bruce took in a sharp breath. He knew that he risked earning a trip to a hellish dimension, but he couldn't help himself.

"Actually, she's not fine," Bruce said. "I watched as she healed completely. There was no long process, no gradual recovery. She was a corpse, burned to the bone, and then, twenty-five seconds later, she was talking to me. If she can heal at that pace, there is no reason that she should be coughing up blood right now besides permanent, deep-tissue damage."

Black Mamba scoffed. "You can't know that. You don't know the first thing about her powers."

Bruce raised his eyebrows. "I notice things. It's kind of what I do."

Quantum-Freak let go of M-80 and walked up to Black Mamba, pleading. "Please. You said that you would help her. I did everything you asked. I was able to open a rift in the exact spot you said, and I brought that thing right from Asgard. I know it took a while, but I did it. I can do exactly what you need, no matter what it ends up being. Please. Just help her."

"You want me to acquiesce to your every need because

you completed the absolute bare minimum of the task I assigned to you?" Black Mamba said. She didn't raise her voice, but her softly spoken words still managed to sting. "I take care of my own. Believe *that*. When you two prove that you deserve to be considered as such, I will make good on my promise. Until then, do what I *say*."

Quantum-Freak went to speak again, but Carmella grabbed her arm, giving her a curt shake of the head. Black Mamba, pretending not to see, motioned for Bruce to come closer to her. With the state of anxiety that Quantum-Freak was in, Bruce knew that he could transform and knock the three of them out before she had a chance to follow through on her threat. But escaping the Serpent Society would be a temporary solution to a larger problem. He'd already learned a great deal about what they were doing—if he stuck it out a little longer, he knew he had a lot more to learn.

And it would start with Quantum-Freak herself.

"Take Banner to the lab. Then find the Avengers. I have to know what they did with the others, and how much they know," Black Mamba said. "If his complexion even changes color in the slightest, send him someplace incredibly *nasty*. The laboratory has cooked up a tranquilizer just for him, but I'd prefer we get our sample before we dose him, if possible."

"Yes, Black Mamba." Quantum-Freak nodded, then grabbed Bruce by the arm and ushered him toward the open door. Bruce watched as she stole one more glance at M-80, who was coughing again as Black Mamba watched.

As Quantum-Freak led him down the metallic hallway lined with bright fluorescent lights, Bruce didn't resist. He walked with her until they reached a staircase. Quantum-Freak let go of him and gave him a slight shove, making him walk first. As he moved onto the first step, he paused, looking down at her from over his shoulder.

"What?" Quantum-Freak snapped. "Move."

Bruce looked her right in the eyes, watching as her cold gaze fell away and was replaced by shining, uncertain eyes. She looked away, then looked back at him, narrowing her eyes, but it was too late. He'd seen it.

"They'll help you," Bruce said. "If you want help, that is. They'll help."

Quantum-Freak leered at him. "*Who*?"

"You're supposed to go after them after you take me wherever I'm going," Bruce said. "You should. They'll help you."

Quantum-Freak stared at him for a moment, before giving him another push. "Shut up and move."

This time, Bruce listened. He was fairly sure that he'd played that moment exactly right—and the best part was, he didn't even have to lie.

The Avengers *would* help her. He just wasn't sure if the help they offered was the help she was looking for.

* * *

Black Mamba stood alone in M-80's holding cell, breathing in sharply through her nose. The girl began to speak, but Black Mamba silenced her with an open-handed strike across the mouth with her gloved palm.

M-80's face jerked to the side. When she turned back to Black Mamba, her pupils blazed with a sudden stream of flames that singed her eyebrows, but there was no anger on her face. Only fear.

She covered her eyes, turning away from Black Mamba. "I—I didn't mean it as a threat. It happens on its own. I swear."

Black Mamba assessed the cowering woman before her. "I'm well aware of how it happens." She reached down, touching M-80's face, which was red and warm from the smack. "And I get the sense that *you* are more aware of your current situation than your significant other."

M-80, her eyes clearing, looked up to meet Mamba's piercing gaze. "Yes."

"When she returns . . . remind her how easily you were given these powers," Mamba said. "I can bestow them upon someone else . . . perhaps someone more grateful . . . with the same ease. You understand that I need a Quantum-Freak and an M-80. I do *not*, however, need an Anita and a Carmella."

"I understand."

"Good," Black Mamba said, turning away from her. "Remain in your cell until I have Puff Adder come for you. I understand you've had a traumatic night, so take the time to calm down. We have big plans ahead."

"But . . . but we were supposed to go meet Benny the Banger," M-80 said. "You said—"

"Different arrangements have been made for the pickup," Black Mamba said. "Rest. Your body *and* your mind. Because I will stress this only once: Quantum-Freak will either fall in line, or you both will die. I welcomed you into my home, and you signed a sacred pact. You will *not* demand recompense from the Serpent Society before you pay your own dues."

"I understand, Black Mamba," M-80 said. "I promise. She'll . . . she'll be fine. I'll show her that everything is going to be fine. I promise."

Without another word, Black Mamba left, slamming the door behind her.

CHAPTER SEVEN

EYE IN THE SKY

"Her name is Anita."

Those were the first words a worn and weary Tony Stark said when he emerged from his elevator, rejoining Natasha, Steve, and Thor in the penthouse of Stark Tower. The room was tinged with pink and gold as the sun rose over the New York City skyline, but with Banner missing in action and Clint in his current state, the mood was decidedly dark. When sharing stories of victorious battles and planning missions, it was easy to pretend that they were old friends gathered for a night of banter and drinks. But life as an Avenger always brought them back down to Earth in the cruelest ways, reminding them just how dangerous their duty was.

Natasha looked up, her eyes wide, her expression unreadable. "How is he?"

Tony waited a beat before answering, and when Natasha didn't follow up with any questions about who Anita was, he sighed, plopping himself down on the couch next to her. "F.R.I.D.A.Y.'s giving me constant updates. Clint is in the infirmary, in and out of consciousness. Constant monitoring. The moment his vitals give even the slightest hint of dropping, F.R.I.D.A.Y. lights this place up. She says that the poison is tough . . . every time the antidote looks like it's beating it, it comes back again, just as strong, as if it was never gone to begin with. I can keep his heart pumping and his lungs going indefinitely, but we need to catch the psycho that did this if we want Clint on his feet. We need a better antidote, one that works specifically for this. And for that, we need more information, because we've got nothing on this poison. Nothing."

The Avengers waited for him to continue.

Tony, just as frustrated as they were, bit his lower lip, shaking his head. "That's all I got."

Natasha closed her eyes, and Steve reached over to squeeze her hand.

"He's going to be okay," Steve said. "Tony, you said 'her name is Anita.' That's Phononeutria?"

"No," Tony said. "Anita is our Ms. MacGuffin, the reason we dove headfirst into this thing at all. I have *all* their names. All five of them. The drones I sent tracking their car—I also had them scan each of these punks for facial recognition during the fight. Each and every one of them is a selfie-taking, Instagram-posting, hashtag-tagging social media addict."

"You speak of hashtags again?" Thor said, raising a brow.

"Don't worry about it, buddy," Tony said. "I'll show you later. I get the feeling you'd be a hashtag-fitspiration guy."

As a perplexed Thor asked Cap to see his phone, Tony leaned over his shoulder and let out a piercing wolf whistle. Moments later, a drone, no bigger than a sparrow, zipped around the room and came to a stop in front of the Avengers. It glowed with repulsor power, hovering silently.

"F.R.I.D.A.Y., give us the exposition," Tony said.

"Yes, sir," F.R.I.D.A.Y.'s voice replied, emanating from the drone. "The woman calling herself 'Quantum-Freak' has been positively identified as Anita Atkinson, twenty-three, of Rockville Centre, New York. A high-school drop-out, Anita is still currently active on three of her six existing social media accounts. She has no known ties to any known criminals, nor have any of her posts, in the distant past all the way through the present, alluded to her having super powers."

"Skip to Phononeutria and the exploding girl," Widow said. "Quantum-Freak may have brought us here, but those are the two who matter right now."

Tony nodded at the drone. "You heard the lady."

"Unlike Anita Atkinson, the woman called 'Phononeutria' *does* have various links to criminals both active and inactive, though none of them have had super powers. Her name is Regina Decker. Thirty-five years old. She has ties to multiple small-time gangs in Staten Island, New York, and has been arrested on charges as severe as armed robbery, assault with a deadly weapon, and attempted murder. While there is nothing on file about her power set, a cursory analysis of the venom found in her stinger matches the venom of the deadliest known araneomorph spider in the world, from which she has taken her name: the *Phoneutria*. Albeit with mystical enhancements we are unable to trace."

Captain America perked up at that bit. "What, was she bitten by a radioactive tarantula?"

"I called Peter Parker after F.R.I.D.A.Y. told me that," Tony said. "Not to generalize our spider-centric friends, but if there's anyone who knows from arachnid-based powers, it's our guy from Queens. No answer. We're keeping on him, though."

F.R.I.D.A.Y. continued: "Her one social media account—a public Facebook—is used exclusively to post links, articles, and videos focusing on conspiracy theories. While she hasn't posted photos herself, the Stark tech ID'd her based on photos in which others have tagged her."

"And the combusting girl?" Thor asked, reaching into a bag of chips.

"Identified as Carmella de Santis, twenty-seven. Also Rockville Centre. Last known residence matches that of Anita Atkinson. She posts to both Instagram and Twitter, though both accounts only feature self-taken images of her and her cats. There have been no posts indicating any ties to crime, nor, like Anita, any indication of super powers. She has extensive medical records and has been in and out of hospitals as far back as we can find, and none of those records show any results that would allude to her having the powers she displayed in tonight's battle, though she has suffered from a variety of debilitating chronic conditions for years. If said conditions are linked to a possible development of super powers, it remains unclear.

"The other two, Deandre and Robert Porter, have both deleted all social media accounts within the last month, but we were able to pull up cached results. While Robert has posted little other than the phrase 'game day!' for the past two years, which lines up with the sporting events of the college at which he matriculated before dropping out, Deandre's Twitter account had been rife with vague references to a big change in his life in the week leading up to its deletion."

"That's a lot of information," Cap said. "I don't want to seem negative here, because the more we know, the better the chance we have of being prepared the next time we go up against these guys . . . but does this get us any closer to finding them?"

"No," Tony said. "I have eyes all over the city, Long Island, and all of the surrounding areas. The moment someone shows up—if they do—F.R.I.D.A.Y. gets a ping."

"Not good enough," Natasha said. "Barton is down and

Banner is missing. I'm not going to sit around waiting for a *ping*. We know they had to be heading somewhere on Long Island—the way they were driving, there's nowhere else they could be going. And without their portal-making friend, they're stuck. We're not doing Clint any good waiting around here—I say we go back and find them ourselves."

"Aye," Thor said. "The tarantula-woman of Staten Island disappeared into the ground with the twins, while Quantum-Freak escaped with the combusting girl into a rift. We can't know where the portal went, but we do know it's likely the groundlings were heading somewhere on Long Island."

"Right," Tony said. "And we can assume that the five of them will meet up at some point. If there's a rendezvous point, the . . . uh 'groundlings,' as Thor so Asgardianly put it, will lead us there."

"Or, maybe we *can* know where the portal went," Black Widow said. "Doctor Strange could help us there, no? He seemed to sense it opening. Maybe he can help us track the other?"

"Makes sense," Tony said. "They're headed toward one place, like you said, Nat. They're strong, but they're sloppy. New. They're going to pop up topside before long, and that's when we'll find them."

"And we should be prepared to do so," Cap said. "Tony, how about you and Thor stick together and look out for Phononeutria and the twins? You two can be an extra set of eyes on top of the drones. Robbie can only mimic powers when he is within range, so we need to hit him with folks who can fly. If Thor can stay out of range once finding them, you have enough power to knock out Robbie from afar, and then it'll be just Phononeutria and Deandre on the ground. Phononeutria can't get past your suit, Tony, and I know Thor took out Deandre last time. Natasha, that leaves us. We'll get in touch with Strange and see where that leads us."

While Tony and Thor prepped to leave, Cap got Stephen Strange on the phone once again. Strange agreed to continue to keep an eye out, and proceeded to send Cap a series of addresses corresponding to mystical disturbances he felt in Long Island.

"These are all over the place," Cap said. "We couldn't follow these on the ground."

"Need someone a bit more aerial than yourselves?" Iron Man asked.

Cap smirked, dialing another number on his cell phone. "Nope. I have someone in mind. And—not that I'm bragging—but I'm willing to bet he'll find our guys quicker than you two."

"Always gotta be a competition," Tony said, grinning at Cap, who flashed him a soft smile.

"Who do you have in mind?" Black Widow asked.

Cap gave a coy shrug. "You could say he's a man with an eye in the sky."

* * *

"Sam Wilson!"

Captain America spread his arms as he approached his old friend, who greeted him with a toothy grin. The two embraced, giving each other a couple of claps on the back.

"You have to do that back-pat thing, or it's not manly enough, right?" Black Widow asked, striding out of the Humvee toward Sam and Cap. Redwing, Sam's falcon, was perched regally on the street sign behind Sam, surveying the area with its dark, keen eyes.

"Not nearly manly enough," Sam said, bringing Natasha in for a hug as well. She gave him a couple of pats on the back before they parted, which earned her a belly laugh.

They were meeting off of the Seaford-Oyster Bay Expressway, where the fight against Quantum-Freak's crew had gone down hours earlier. Like Cap and Widow, Sam was suited up for battle, donning his red and white armor, complete with a set of wings that matched the color of his falcon. These wings had once been jet powered, but his uniform and flight harness had since been upgraded with holographic hard-light wings, which came from a field generator strapped to his back. Operated with a cybernetic link, this upgrade allowed Sam to control the size of his wingspan instantaneously, giving him complete autonomy over his flight.

Sam Wilson was the Falcon, an Avenger, and one of Captain America's best friends. And today, Cap was calling in a favor.

"This is going to be a fun one, isn't it?" Sam said. His eyes were obscured by dark lenses, but Cap knew Sam well enough that he could picture the excited gleam that was surely behind the shades. "What are we doing, infiltrating a Hydra stronghold? Taking out Skrull overlords posing as politicians? Breaking up a monster monster-truck rally?"

"Actually," Steve said, creasing his brow, "I was kind of hoping to borrow Redwing."

Sam looked at Cap, the excitement immediately gone. "You wanna borrow my falcon."

"I kind of want to borrow your falcon, yes."

Sam turned to Redwing, spreading his arms in disbelief. "You hearing this? Cap wants to talk to you, buddy. I guess I could've stayed home. Caught up on my shows."

"I wouldn't go *that* far," Widow said as Redwing flew over, landing on Sam's outstretched arm. "Cap definitely needed that glorious man hug. It's been a hard day."

"Yeah?" Sam asked. "Everything okay?"

"We're hoping you can help us find out," Cap said. "Bruce Banner is missing. He was taken into a rip in the fabric of reality by a woman calling herself 'Quantum-Freak.' Real name Anita Atkinson. Now, because Anita's girlfriend was also thrown into the rift, we have no reason to believe that

Anita would purposely endanger them *both* ... so we're hoping that Redwing can help us find Bruce, or at least Anita."

Sam looked to Redwing, who cocked his head. Speaking silently to the bird through their telepathic link, Sam cocked his own head to the side and narrowed his eyes. Redwing turned toward Captain America and took flight, then landed softly on his shoulder.

"He knows Bruce, of course. Show him whatever you've got on Anita. Her girlfriend, too," Sam said. "If there's anyone on this globe that'll find them, it's Redwing."

"I know," Cap said, looking toward Redwing with genuine admiration. "The problem is, we already have Iron Man's drones on the lookout ... and we're coming up with nothing. No leads, no possible locations other than *somewhere* on Long Island, east of this location."

"Not much to go on, is what you're saying," Sam said.

"What we do have is help from Stephen Strange," Cap said. "He's keeping his senses peeled for any local mystical blips. He's texted me a list of places so far ... and he's saying that this could really be anything. The magical world interacts with our own reality constantly, so this isn't going on much, but it's the best we have."

"Let's see what you've got," Sam said.

Black Widow stood in front of Sam and Redwing, scrolling through the pictures F.R.I.D.A.Y. had found of Anita and Carmella. After looking at the images, Sam turned to Cap, who gave him the list of locations from Doctor Strange. As Sam read it aloud, Redwing closed his eyes, as if silently memorizing the list.

Sam finished the list and, without a moment of pause, Redwing launched off of Cap's shoulder, taking off into the early morning sky with a high-pitched cry that echoed long after the bird had disappeared from sight.

"If anyone can find them, Redwing will," Sam said. He looked toward the sky, which was clear and bright. "What do we do until then?"

Black Widow, her tone deadly, said, "We wait. We get ready. Because when we find them, we're going to take them *down*."

* * *

After an hour of high-speed flying around eastern Long Island with no luck, Thor and Iron Man landed on the roof of a burger joint for a break. It wasn't open for a few more hours, so there was no one to gawk at the two Avengers sitting on top of the roof, which was shaped to look like an anthropomorphized burger—pickles for eyes and an arc of ketchup for a smile—waving prospective customers in with a French-fry arm. Tony thought it was rather unnerving himself, but when they settled in, he heard Thor's stomach let out a thunderous rumble, so he supposed it did the trick.

"I confess, Stark . . . I have no idea what in Odin's stones we're looking for," Thor said wistfully, staring out at the cloudless sky.

"I don't . . . wait, what? Odin's *what*?"

"Merely an expression," Thor said, with a shrug.

"We're looking for three idiots to pop up out of the ground, so we can knock 'em back down," Tony replied.

"You and I both could fly across this entire state in the time it would take me to hail a taxi in New York," Thor said. "This method of searching is foolhardy, and will prove fruitless. Your F.R.I.D.A.Y. is our best hope at any leads. It would better serve us to regroup at Stark Tower and watch over our fallen comrade."

"He isn't *fallen*," Tony said. "He's going to be fine. And I have an entire armory protecting him, with F.R.I.D.A.Y. offering him better on-location care than any of us could. Anyone short of Banner, anyway."

"Do you think we will find these villains with our naked eye?"

Tony turned to Thor, his face mask snapping up to reveal weary eyes. "No. But I'd rather spend my time searching than sitting on the bench. Same goes for most of us."

Thor assessed him, rubbing his square, stubbly chin with his huge hand. "You should take care of yourself, Stark. The shadow of the night hides it well, but the light of day reveals much. The bags under your eyes grow darker every time we meet."

"Bags?" Tony said, snickering. "Last time I looked, I had a whole shopping spree under there."

"Even those whom the people of Earth once called *gods* must rest," Thor said. "What keeps you up these days, Stark?"

Tony began to answer, but paused, realizing, for the first time in a long time, that he had no idea what he was going to say. He looked at Thor, cocking his brow. "You know . . . I honestly don't know. My armor is functioning better than ever. I hesitate to use the word perfect, because the moment I start doing that is the moment I'll want to tear it all down and start from scratch. Prove myself wrong. Do better. But . . . Iron Man is in a good place. It's almost as if . . ."

Thor frowned, waiting for Stark to continue.

"This is gonna sound messed up," Tony said. "But as soon as Clint called . . . 'Tony, the sky's opening up, spitting out rhino-slugs.' I . . . heh. I didn't even process the fact that I thought it, but I did. I did. I thought, *Finally*. Finally something. And now, here we are, two men down and in a stranger situation than I could've ever predicted. And . . ."

"And now you have a reason to stay up," Thor said.

"'Cause I sure as hell can't sleep anyway."

Thor flipped Mjolnir in his hand. "Believe it or not, Stark, I understand. As a boy . . . the idea of a peaceful day was torturous. Part of me would rather an army lay siege to my father's kingdom than face the thought of whiling away a weekend of leisure. At least, then, I'd have something to hit."

"Hah," Tony said, leaning back on the gigantic burger. "And here I thought I was a freak show."

"Oh, you most certainly are," Thor said. "You're just not alone."

The two of them started to laugh together, but Tony tensed up when his helmet slammed shut and his HUD lit up with footage from one of his drones. He stood, holding out a hand to Thor signaling him to silence his booming laughter.

"Phononeutria, along with Robbie and Deandre Porter, have been spotted breaching the ground near Belmont Lake State Park," F.R.I.D.A.Y. said, as Tony watched the drone's feed. It was a bird's-eye view of three people, caked in dirt from head to toe, stumbling down a dirt path that circled a lake.

Tony looked at Thor, the eyes of his mask lighting up with bright blue power as he prepared to take off. "Got 'em. Do me a favor, Thor . . . remember the time. 6:32 a.m."

"6:32 a.m.," Thor repeated. "Why?"

"Cap thinks his buddy's *bird* is faster than my drones?" Iron Man said. "If the man wants to challenge me, I accept. I bet I won."

"You are indeed a freak show, Tony Stark," Thor said.

"Yeah, well. At least I'm self-aware," Tony said. "Now . . . how about we get off this burger and go show these three punks just how much guys like us don't like to sit around and wait?"

"Let's," Thor said, and the two of them, side by side, blasted off into the open sky, leaving the pickle-eyed burger waving at them with its fry hand.

* * *

Back at Stark Tower, Clint jolted awake for the third time that hour, taking in a deep, gulping breath. He tried to move his arms, but found that he was strapped to the gurney in Tony's infirmary, tubes feeding different color fluids into each of his arms. No matter how often he slipped out of consciousness only to wake up again, being unable to move his limbs was a shock every time. Worse, his blood felt like it was scalding his veins, sending surges of hot, white pain through his body every time he awoke, making his vision quiver before him. He wondered how much agony he could take before his body shut down again. Usually, by the time he had that thought, he was moments away from passing out once more. Tony had been smart to strap him down, though; he knew Clint well. If he had been free to move, he would've instinctually stood upon waking, and he would've passed out again on the infirmary floor.

There was something different about this time, though. Clint couldn't turn his head enough to see to the far left of the room, but from the corner of his eye, he saw a blot of red energy move across the air. At first, he thought that

Tony, clad in the Iron Man armor, might have walked into the room, but as the red energy expanded in the ceiling, he knew that he was wrong.

"Oh, no," he said, his voice hoarse, unrecognizable to his own ears. "Oh *no no no*. No freakin' way!"

He strained against the straps as the red energy tore a hole in the center of the room. He looked around, hoping that one of the other Avengers was racing down to the infirmary to stop whatever came out of this portal from devouring him. He prayed that it wasn't another Barglewarf—if he was going to die, he couldn't help but think that that thing had far too ridiculous a name to be the thing that killed him.

But what stepped out of the portal was neither slimy nor foul. Quantum-Freak, her eyes wild and bloodshot, appeared from the darkness of the world that lay behind her power, moving toward Clint with purpose.

"Natasha!" Clint bellowed, thrashing on his gurney to no avail. "Tony! Thor! Steve! I'm strapped down here! I've got a *problem*!"

Just as Quantum-Freak was within a yard of Clint, an unmanned Iron Man armor—Clint knew it was drone operated, as he recognized it as an old model—flew into the room, its gauntlets lit up with repulsor energy, ready to send Quantum-Freak blasting through the wall. In the distance, Clint could hear the robotic whine of what he knew was an army of suits of Tony's armor coming to his defense, flooding up from the armory.

Not for the first time, Clint *really* appreciated being friends with the smartest man in the world.

Clint's relief was short lived, though. As the armor sped toward Quantum-Freak, she waved her hands, and the red, crackling portal shot at the suit like a bolt of lightning. Before it could even send the repulsor beam at her, it was enveloped in her portal, which closed as soon as it swallowed the armor whole.

As Clint struggled against the straps, Quantum-Freak closed the distance between them. She reached out and, with a warm, powerful hand, grabbed Clint's throat. She bore down on him, her eyes sparkling with red power, her touch sending static shocks into his flesh, making his hair stand up.

"Don't try *anything*," Quantum-Freak said through gritted teeth. "And, so help me, don't pass out."

"Really trying to not do that," Clint said. "The choking isn't helping."

A repulsor beam shot toward Quantum-Freak, who ducked, letting out a grunt. As what looked like an endless army of suits barreled toward the entrance to the infirmary, Quantum-Freak lashed out both hands. The door, along with the entire area surrounding it, exploded with red energy. She swiped her hands across the air in front of her, and the energy opened up into a portal, preventing the drone-operated suits from getting into the room.

"I'm *not* here to hurt anyone," she screamed. "Back down before I start regretting this!"

Clint looked up at the glowing woman, not even the slightest bit comforted by her words. She turned to him, placing her hand back on his throat.

"You're dying," Quantum-Freak said. "Whatever they're doing, it won't help. Phononeutria's venom is going to start to multiply. Slowly, at first. And then, just as you begin to feel as if you can't breathe, the water in your body will turn to acid. After that, it'll be quick. Ish."

"Why are you telling me this?"

"Because you have three options," Quantum-Freak said, loosening her grip on Clint's neck. "You can die that way. Excruciating, relentless, bloody."

"Whatever the rest of the options are, I'll take 'em over that," Clint said. He took in a deep breath, wondering if his lungs were starting to tighten, or if he was imagining it.

"Second option," Quantum-Freak said, "is that you help me. If you do—and I make no guarantees—I will try my very best to make sure you live through this."

"Yeah, okay. Sure. And if I don't?"

"That leads us to the third option," Quantum-Freak said, her eyes flashing red. "I'll kill you right here, right now."

CHAPTER EIGHT

LEAP OF FAITH

Iron Man and Thor hovered about one-hundred feet above the park below, unseen by the dirt-covered trio that was approaching the end of the joggers' path below. The heroes watched their targets pass a group of civilians who were walking their dogs. The animals erupted into fits of barking as they crossed the three grimy villains. Thor tensed when he saw Phononeutria lift an arm, as if preparing to launch her stingers at one of the passing dogs, but Deandre pulled her away before she could act, shaking his head.

"She was about to kill that dog," Iron Man said. "Did you see that?"

"Oh, I saw that," Thor said, clenching his jaw.

The trio walked on, brushing dirt off themselves as they trudged, leaving a trail of brown dust behind them.

"We're in the clear," Iron Man said. "Who gets to do the honors?"

"Shall we play the rock, the paper, and the scissors?" Thor asked, hooking the loop on the end of Mjolnir to his belt.

"You're on," Iron Man said. "We going 'shoot' or 'says shoot'?"

"Hawkeye taught me 'says shoot,' and so shall it be."

As Phononeutria, Deandre, and Robbie reached the end of the path and turned onto an empty street, shaking off dirt with every step, Iron Man and Thor pounded their hands in their fists in the skies above.

"Rock, paper, scissors says . . ." they said in unison. "Shoot!"

They tossed out their hands. Iron Man's gauntlet was opened flat, while Thor stuck out two fingers from his meaty fist.

"A foolish choice," Thor proclaimed. "Scissors beat paper!"

"Two out of three."

"I am afraid not," Thor said as he turned toward the three below and unhooked Mjolnir. He spun the hammer over his head until it became a blur, the sky quickly darkening in response as storm clouds gathered. Phononeutria only looked up once an earth-shaking eruption of thunder followed a flash of lightning, but by the time she locked eyes with a grinning Thor, who was descending to the ground near them, it was too late.

Thor's hand was empty.

Mjolnir arced down and then back toward Thor, knocking Phononeutria in the temple and slamming Deandre in the forehead, sending his skull smacking into Robbie's—all lightly enough to keep them from having any real damage, but roughly enough to knock them out for a good while. As the hammer completed its circle, moving back into Thor's open hand, the three fell to the ground at once, producing a cloud of dirt.

"You know, you should just do that every time to everyone," Iron Man said, flying down to the ground alongside of Thor, who, grinning devilishly, wiped a smudge off of his hammer.

As they landed before the fallen trio, Iron Man's HUD lit up with a red flash, and he was suddenly looking at the camera feed from the infirmary at Stark Tower. Anita Atkinson—Quantum-Freak herself—hovered over Clint Barton, her hand on his throat.

"There has been a security breach!" F.R.I.D.A.Y.'s voice said. "Five drone-operated suits have already been damaged, and the entrance to the infirmary has been transformed into an open rift, but upon your command, we can enter through the—"

"Don't wait for my command!" Tony barked. "Clint's in there alone! Light her up. I'm on the way."

Thor looked down at the unconscious Phononeutria, Robbie, and Deandre. "Go. Contact S.H.I.E.L.D. for a pickup on your way. I can handle these three until then."

Tony looked at Thor, his eye slits glowing as he prepared to take off. "If they wake up?"

"I pray they do," Thor said. "I'd relish the chance to show them just how annoyed I am."

Iron Man took off into the sky like a bullet, disappearing into the clouds above in an instant.

* * *

Quantum-Freak stared down at Clint Barton, who was struggling to stay conscious. The room was spinning, blurry, pulsating. Clint feared that he was further along toward the end than Quantum-Freak knew. His lungs were tight, and tingled with what reminded Clint of intense heartburn. He knew very well that he could be imagining it, driven to fear the worst because of Quantum-Freak's graphic explanation of what would happen to his body . . . but the alternative was that the water in his body was about to eat through his flesh.

Clint was a survivor. He wasn't going to risk it.

"I'll help you," he croaked. "I don't know how you expect me to lift a finger when I can barely open my mouth right now, but hey. I'll see what I can do."

"This is the Avengers stronghold, right?" Quantum-Freak asked, removing her hand from Clint's throat. "I came here looking for them. I figured if . . . if I came in peace, you all might . . ."

"*This* was coming in peace?"

Quantum-Freak sighed, knitting her fingers together

nervously. "I shouldn't be doing this. They'll kill me. *And her.*"

"You're babbling, and I'm about twenty-five percent awake right now," Clint said. "What are you looking to do?"

Without warning, the ceiling behind Quantum-Freak exploded in a beam of repulsor energy. A series of Iron Man drones followed it, zipping into the room as Quantum-Freak's face flooded with panic. Letting out a nervous cry, she threw herself to the ground as repulsor energy rained down on her. The portal blocking the door came down, and even more Iron Man suits flowed into the room, all of them training their glowing gauntlets on the fallen Quantum-Freak.

"Stand down," they all said at once, speaking with F.R.I.D.A.Y.'s voice.

Quantum-Freak held up her hands, her eyes wide. "Like I said. I'm not here for trouble. I want to make a deal."

"You say that, but this *looks* quite a bit like trouble to me," F.R.I.D.A.Y. replied.

"Let her talk," Clint said. "Back off a bit. I mean, still blast the crap out of her if she tries to choke me again . . . but we were just getting to the part where she makes my body not turn to acid. I liked that part."

Quantum-Freak stood, nervously eyeing the Iron Man suits that seemed to glare at her with their glowing, robotic eyes.

"Where are the rest of the Avengers?" Quantum-Freak said, adopting a forced note of authority to her voice. "If *they* help me, I'll make sure you survive this. If even one of them is out, no deal. Understood?"

"Sure," Clint croaked. "Understood, yeah."

"So, where *are* they?" Quantum-Freak urged.

Clint couldn't help but let out a snicker. "You just opened a portal in Tony Stark's home, sending some of his suits to who *knows* where. If you think he wasn't aware of that the second your foot touched his floor, then you have no idea who you're dealing with. You can bet they're on their way."

"Actually, I'm here already. Hi."

Clint grinned upon hearing Tony Stark's voice from across the room. He watched as Quantum-Freak spun around to face the Iron Man suits, unable to pick out which one was piloted by the real Tony Stark. The cluster of drones parted as Iron Man himself, in the latest armor, strode into the room, face mask lifted to reveal Tony's face.

He looked unimpressed.

Stark's voice spoke through all of the suits at once. "Magic hands where I can see them. Go on. Put 'em up again."

Quantum-Freak clenched her fists, her eyes darting from Iron Man to Clint, as if trying to decide if she would be better off listening or attempting to fight. Then, slowly, she opened her hands and lifted them into the air, letting out a deep breath.

"Good move," Tony said. "Now, tell me what I should do with you. You trashed five of my suits, so from where I'm standing, we've got property damage at the amount of . . . including the holes in the infirmary, we're looking at about six hundred million. Fair?"

"You're joking," Quantum-Freak said, seething.

"Yeah," Tony said. "But trust me. I'm not laughing. You've done a lot of damage in the short time I've been aware of your existence. What's my move here?"

"She says she wants to help," Clint said, wheezing.

"I heard," Tony said. "You believe her?"

Clint groaned. "You heard that bit about acid, man?"

Tony nodded, his eyes locked on Quantum-Freak, who held her arms skyward. Sighing, he waved the drone-operated suits away. Following his movements, they moved out of the doorway, making a path for Quantum-Freak. "Allow my friends here to accompany you to the penthouse. I'll take the quick way. Through the hole you made me make in my ceiling."

Quantum-Freak consented, and strode out of the room, followed by her escort of Iron Man suits. Clint breathed a sigh of relief, and felt a distinctly acidic burn in his throat. He let out a sputtering cough, silently hoping that whatever conversation Quantum-Freak and Iron Man had would happen quickly.

Iron Man stood over Clint, his face creased with concern. "You think she's telling the truth?"

Clint looked up at Tony and shrugged. He didn't have to say another word. Iron Man looked away and jumped up through the hole his drones had made in the ceiling, leaving Clint alone with his pain.

* * *

As Quantum-Freak was ushered into the penthouse by the drone-operated Iron Man armors, Tony Stark was already walking across the room from the other side, munching on a handful of chips. He held the bag out to Quantum-Freak as the other suits walked away from her, heading back toward the elevator.

"Chip?"

Quantum-Freak shook her head, standing awkwardly before Iron Man. He stared at her blankly.

"Should I . . . sit?"

"I don't know," Tony said. "I *did* invite you to the penthouse, so that kind of makes you a guest. On the other hand, though, you also just broke into my home and choked my dying friend, which makes me a bit less hospitable. So, yeah. How about you stand."

Quantum-Freak frowned. "Fair."

"We've had eyes on you since the fight," Tony said. "Anita Atkinson. What brings a person like you into conflict with the Avengers, ripping portals open all over New

York? Standing alongside a walking, talking landfill like Phononeutria?"

"People do crazy things for their loved ones."

Tony lifted his brows, then put aside his bag of chips. "They sure do. Which brings me to Clint Barton. Close friend of mine. Great guy. Not in a good state at the moment, though. Not that *your* guys are, for that matter. The mighty Thor—you remember him—has the rest of your buddies in custody, and they're about to get sent off to S.H.I.E.L.D. for processing. Thing is, I'm willing to bet Phononeutria won't willingly help us fix Clint, which is a problem."

"You're right," Quantum-Freak said. "She'd never."

"I hear *you* have a problem, too."

Her jaw tensed. "I do."

"Taking an educated guess here," Tony said. "It has to do with your atomic bomb of a girlfriend. Carmella. That has to be a hard life. In and out of hospitals, closer relationship with your doctor than just about anyone. That kinda thing could drive a person to some pretty radical choices. Am I wrong?"

"How do you know that?" she asked. "How do you know any of this?"

Tony raised a brow. "You know who we *are* right?"

Quantum-Freak stood across from Iron Man, her heart racing, knowing that whatever she said next would mean she was taking a step into the unknown. She'd felt the same way when she and Carmella were approached by Black Mamba for the first time with that seemingly impossible offer. Now, she stood across from a man that she was supposed to hate, knowing that whatever she said would determine the course of her and Carmella's lives. After all, he was already a step ahead of her, to put it lightly.

She could still escape. She could open up a portal and never look back, and put her faith completely in Black Mamba. Maybe she really could save Carmella. Maybe that was the only way.

Quantum-Freak closed her eyes, making her choice.

"Yes," she said. "Carmella . . . you're right. She's dying."

"So we're in the same boat then," Tony said. "You don't want your girlfriend to die. I don't want my buddy to die."

"I'll help you," Quantum-Freak said, her chin trembling. "I promise. Just . . . please. I don't know what to do. I messed up, and now . . . now it's worse than ever."

"Who's pulling the strings here?"

"I—"

"Nope," Tony said, shaking his head. "This is step one. Tell me. Right now. Who are we up against?"

Quantum-Freak swallowed, looking off to the side. The words seemed to slip out of her mouth. "The Serpent Society."

Tony assessed Quantum-Freak with his dark, unreadable gaze. After what seemed like an eternity, the face mask snapped shut, and the eye slits came alive with blue light.

"Can you fly?" he asked.

"What? No."

"Figured. So, here is where *I* take a leap of faith," Tony said. "Because I believe that you really do want our help, and I'm going to give you the chance to earn it. How about you and I take a stroll through one of those portals of yours?"

* * *

"Redwing has something," Falcon said.

Captain America, who sat next to him in the back of the Humvee alongside of Black Widow, watched as his friend closed his eyes, his lips moving slowly as he telepathically communicated with Redwing. Steve often wondered what it was like for Sam, to have that link to another living being, a connection beyond friendship, beyond individuality. A bond unlike any other. The closest thing that Cap had to that was his friendship with Bucky Barnes, but as close as they were, there were times that he would watch Bucky fall deep into thought, or perhaps memory, lost to the world. In those private moments, Cap couldn't begin to guess what Bucky was thinking. He wondered if, because of that link to Redwing, Sam felt less alone in the world than the rest of them did.

Falcon nodded, and then turned to Captain America and Black Widow. "It's not Bruce. We're not even sure if it's related. But Redwing got a glimpse of something mighty strange not far from your throwdown this morning. Strange has that location pegged with more mystical disturbances than any not only in the area, but in the state."

"What is it?" Captain America asked.

"Steve . . . when was the last time you went head to head with the Serpent Society?" Falcon asked.

Cap rubbed his chin. "Haven't heard a word from them in . . . upward of a year, maybe a year and a half."

"Longer than that for me," Widow added.

"Well, get this. Redwing just caught Copperhead meeting off of the Sagtikos State Parkway with some pretty strange bedfellows," Falcon said. Copperhead was a high-ranking member of the Serpent Society, one who had often worked in the past under its various leaders, doing their dirty work. Sam continued: "Do you two know Benny the Banger?"

"Thankfully, this is the first time I've ever heard anyone say that name," Widow said.

"Also goes by Grand Slam, the Bronx Bomber . . . I could go on," Falcon said. "Guy has more nicknames than he has fingers. He's a mobster out of New York. He works as Maggia muscle. From what I know, he's not big time or anything, but he's got a nasty reputation for beating folks with baseball bats. What would bring a guy like *that* to meet with a member of the Serpent Society, I have no idea. Figured it could be worth looking into."

"Absolutely," Cap said. "You wouldn't happen to know *who* he works under, would you?"

"I'm not one-hundred percent, but I think he's a Paulie Chase guy. Could be wrong," Sam said.

Cap looked up, meeting Black Widow's eyes. They may not have had a telepathic connection, but he knew Natasha well enough to know *exactly* what she was thinking.

"Good work, Sam," Cap said. "Does Redwing still have eyes on Copperhead?"

"You bet."

"Tell F.R.I.D.A.Y. the location and have the Humvee reroute to take us after him," Cap said. "We found Paulie Chase murdered in his home last night, and I'm starting to wonder if Quantum-Freak's team is involved."

"You've already told me," F.R.I.D.A.Y. said. "I can hear everything you're saying."

Cap looked sheepishly at a smirking Natasha and shrugged.

"My question is, where does the Serpent Society factor in to all of this?" Black Widow asked.

"I'm wondering the same thing," Captain America said as the Humvee pulled a U-turn and took off toward Copperhead. If they were right about this latest development, and there was a connection between these seemingly random events, they might be facing a much vaster conspiracy than they'd imagined. If the Serpent Society was joining forces with New York City's underground crime syndicate, two minor but consistent nuisances were on their way to becoming a big, big problem.

The thought troubled Cap, but if it led them closer to finding out where Bruce Banner had been taken, he would gladly face whatever was waiting for him on the other side of this mystery.

* * *

Thor sat on the empty bleachers of North Babylon High School's football field, staring at the writhing forms of Phononeutria and Robbie. Deandre was laid out on the bleachers next to Thor, unconscious. Thor had ripped off the railing of the bleachers and used it as a makeshift set of handcuffs, bending it around Phononeutria, Deandre, and Robbie's arms while they were still passed out. As long as he maintained distance from them, Robbie couldn't mimic his moves and Phononeutria couldn't reach him with her stingers.

"You can't keep us here forever!" Phononeutria screamed across the field. "The people we work for will find you!"

Thor rolled his eyes. She had been shouting threats across the field since she had woken up, her arms and legs bound by the twisted metal pole. Thor had decided that the field would be the best place to keep the three villains until

S.H.I.E.L.D. arrived to take them in to custody; it was large enough to allow Thor to keep an eye on them without getting too close and, with school out for the summer, it was relatively secluded.

The God of Thunder, however, grew bored. And, even more pressingly, he grew *hungry*. He closed his eyes, thinking fondly of the gigantic burger upon which he and Tony Stark had sat. Thor silently made a plan to stop for a few burgers at that very location when all of this was over.

As he daydreamed about the various toppings he would get, the sky above the field lit up with a red surge of energy, which sped toward the ground like a bolt of lightning. As it careened toward the grass, it ripped the sky open in a red, blazing gash, as if it had unzipped reality itself.

Thor instantly took flight and held Mjolnir up to the clouds, ready to toss the hammer at the first sign of Quantum-Freak. Phononeutria was cackling triumphantly, rolling around on the ground as she looked at the portal hungrily.

"I warned you!" Phononeutria screamed. "It's all bad now!"

Something moved in the darkness of the portal, and Thor prepared to release the hammer. But it wasn't Quantum-Freak who stepped out of the pulsing hole in the sky at first. It was Iron Man.

Thor let out a hearty laugh as Phononeutria's grin withered on her face.

"Shellhead!" Thor cried out, waving to him with the hammer. "I almost reduced you to scrap metal!"

Iron Man looked toward the sky and saluted Thor. "Yeah, yeah. I'm too fast for you, anyway."

Then, to deepen Thor's confusion, another figure emerged from the portal, which closed behind her as she stepped onto the field: Quantum-Freak herself. Thor looked from Iron Man to Quantum-Freak and back again.

"Should I . . ." Thor made a striking motion with his hammer.

Iron Man shook his head. "We're good on the smiting. For now." He turned to Quantum-Freak. "Talk to her, now. S.H.I.E.L.D. is already en route, and if you're still here when they arrive, I won't be able to stop them from taking you, too. Well, I would be *able* to. I just wouldn't."

"Bring her to me," Quantum-Freak said. "If I get too close, Robbie could shadow my power."

"Clever girl," Iron Man said. He blasted over to Phononeutria and grabbed her by her arm, looking at the metal pole wrapped around her limbs. "Thor. Dude. Did you tie a *fence* around her?"

"Let *GO* of me!" Phononeutria snapped. She let out a series of stingers, which clattered ineffectually against Iron Man's armor.

"Merely a railing," Thor corrected.

"We'll bill it to S.H.I.E.L.D.," Tony said, dragging a raging

Phononeutria over to Quantum-Freak. "You really pretzeled this thing."

When they were far enough away from Robbie, Iron Man deposited Phononeutria in front of Quantum-Freak. He held out his gauntlet, his repulsor energy putting a spotlight on her.

Phononeutria was caked with dirt, her hair jutting out wildly, her eyes bloodshot from pure rage. She leered at Tony, her arms beginning to glow as she prepared a new series of stingers.

"Yikes," Tony said, withdrawing from her a bit. "Not your best moment."

"Traitor!" she hissed at Quantum-Freak.

"Keep those nasty things to yourself," Quantum-Freak said. She waved her hands, and a new portal opened up on the ground between herself and Phononeutria with a wave of red energy. Phononeutria was right on the edge of the portal—if it expanded so much as a foot, she would tilt right in. "Remember that place I was telling you about when we first met? The world on the other side of the veil . . . the one that gave me nightmares?"

Phononeutria gulped as a screeching roar came from within. A sound that initially seemed like thunder drew nearer, and Thor realized that what he heard was a gigantic set of wings flapping.

"This portal leads there. Do *not* make me send you there, Regina."

Thor landed next to Iron Man, nodding his head.

"I don't know what happened with her since we last spoke, but I like her much better now," Thor said.

"She's not half-bad," Tony said. "Well, sure, she's literally half bad, but still."

"What are you *doing*?" Phononeutria rasped. "They'll kill you."

"Give me the antidote," Quantum-Freak demanded. "Now."

"You're out of your mind," Phononeutria spat back at her. "They'll kill *me*! Do you know what they've done for us? How could you turn your back on them like this, after everything they've given you?"

"The *antidote*," Quantum-Freak snapped. She clenched her fist, and the portal inched toward Phononeutria. For a moment, it appeared that Phononeutria would allow herself to fall . . . but then, she jerked her shoulder to the side to roll away from the opening.

"Fine . . ." she said. "Fine. But I will make sure *they* know . . ." The glow in her arms shifted from red to a sickly yellow, and then, to a pulsing green. Her skin opened in a series of deep slits, and Thor prepared to strike her with Mjolnir once again as saw stingers begin to push themselves out of her widening pores, but Iron Man held up a hand to stop him.

Instead of stingers, five spongelike orbs, glowing green under a thick layer of mucous, popped out of her flesh and rolled across the grass, leaving a trail of slime in their wake.

Quantum-Freak, her nose wrinkled, picked up each one of the orbs and stuffed them into her hoodie. She walked over to Thor, holding out her hand for him to shake.

"Sorry about before," Quantum-Freak said. "I really didn't want to fight. I kinda had to keep the mission secret from the Avengers, ooooor my boss would've . . . you know, literally cut our heads off."

Thor looked at her hand, which dripped with slime, and offered his fist. "Pound this," Thor said. Quantum-Freak raised a brow, but punched Thor's fist anyway.

"*It*," Iron Man said. "Pound it."

"Right, yes. I said that," Thor said.

Quantum-Freak looked over her shoulder, back at Phononeutria, who was trying her best to roll away from the active portal. "You know, if you guys wanted, I could still knock her in there. She's one of my bottom five people I've ever met. I wouldn't lose any sleep over it."

Tony and Thor exchanged a glance, as if they were considering it, but both then offered a series of halfhearted "No"s and "We couldn't"s and "It would be wrong"s.

"What lies beyond the rift anyway?" Thor said. The thunderous sound of the flapping wings was louder than ever.

Quantum-Freak shook her head and closed the portal with a wave of her hand. "Hope that you never find out."

"Come on," Tony said moments later when they saw a S.H.I.E.L.D. helicopter descending. "We're going back to the tower. Once Clint is okay, you're going to tell us everything. *Everything.* Are we on the same page?"

Quantum-Freak looked at the approaching helicopter with wide eyes. "Yes."

"They're not going to take you as long as you're with us," Iron Man said.

She nodded. "Okay."

Iron Man motioned for Quantum-Freak to open another portal back to Stark Tower. Having already given S.H.I.E.L.D. Director Maria Hill the necessary warnings regarding Phononeutria's, Robbie's, and Deandre's powers, Iron Man strode into the portal.

Quantum-Freak motioned for Thor to follow him.

"No," he said. "You first."

"What? The God of Thunder is scared?" she asked.

"Never," Thor replied. "The God of Thunder is cautious."

Quantum-Freak stared at Thor, his cape billowing in the wind as the helicopter descended.

"I . . . was not aware of how pathetic that was going to sound. Into the portal it is," Thor said, and proceeded into the rift, followed closely by Quantum-Freak, who left her former allies behind on the football field. Thor still had no idea who they were, or who Quantum-Freak was for that matter, nor what their plan was, but to his eye, it seemed that they now had a way to save Clint's life. For the moment, that was all that mattered.

CHAPTER NINE

ORIGIN STORY

Clint still looked like the walking dead, but at least he was walking.

Tony, back in his T-shirt and sweats, sat on the infirmary table where Clint had been hooked up to the intravenous system moments before. He had been unconscious when Tony, Thor, and Anita had returned, and was being tended to by F.R.I.D.A.Y.'s watchful eye—but his condition had clearly worsened. Anita force-fed him the slimy spheres that had popped out of Phononeutria's arms. As she held her hand over Clint's mouth, he'd broken into another fit of seizures, just as he had when he'd first been stung. For a horrible second, Tony thought that Phononeutria had produced an even deadlier poison in the guise of an antidote, and that they'd all been duped, but his fear broke when Clint's convulsions stopped and his eyes opened. He'd blinked at them and asked: "What the hell did you just stuff in my mouth?"

Now, he was buttoning up a shirt that he'd borrowed from Tony, a little worse for the wear, but alive to tell the tale. Anita and Thor had moved up to the penthouse while waiting for Clint to clean up, but Tony had stayed with him in the infirmary.

"How are you feeling?" Tony asked as Clint looked at himself in the mirror on the side of the room.

"Not nearly as bad as I look," Clint said, turning on the sink faucet below the mirror. He filled his hands with a pool of water. "Could go for coffee. And none of that K-Cup crap. I want a pot."

"Pot of coffee it is," Tony said. "You hear that, F.R.I.D.A.Y.? We're headed to the penthouse. Two pots. One for Clint, one for everyone else."

"Heh. I thought for a second that you were actually going to brew it yourself," Clint said. He doused his face with water, rubbing his eyes.

"What am I, a Neanderthal? Do you think I drive a stone car?"

Clint shook the excess water off of his hands. "What do you think about the girl up there? Someone we can trust?"

"I think she's asking the same about us," Tony said.

Clint bobbed his head. "I might be dead if she didn't feed me . . . the hell were those things again? Brussels sprouts dipped in garbage juice, right? Because I feel like my tongue will never be the same. Not to complain. Because . . . you know, I'm here."

"Hey, F.R.I.D.A.Y., let's also get some mints for Clint."

"I'll stick to the coffee," Clint said as they walked into the hall.

"Listen, I'm glad you're alive. But trust me when I say this: those mints are for everyone else in the room," Tony said. "Do me a favor and eat them."

"Fair," Clint said.

As they got in the elevator and headed up to the penthouse, Tony snapped his fingers. "Oh, wow. Hey. F.R.I.D.A.Y. Give Cap a call." He turned to Clint, shrugging. "Completely forgot to tell them that you're not a corpse."

A few rings later, Steve Rogers's voice answered, playing through the speaker system in the elevator. "Tony. Any update?"

"I have someone here who wants to say 'Hi,'" Tony said.

Clint let out a long sigh. "Hey, Cap."

"Clint?" Captain America asked, the excitement clear in his voice.

There was the sound of movement on the line, and then Black Widow's voice sounded over the system, urgent and intense. "Barton, tell me that you're okay."

"I'm okay, Nat."

There was a beat of silence on the other side. When Natasha spoke again, her voice was softer. "It's very good to hear your voice."

"All right, everyone's good, everyone's alive," Tony said, turning away from Clint to hide his smile. "We've still got a long day's journey into night ahead of us. Got a hell of an update for you, too. Clearly. Anything on your end?"

As the elevator rose to the penthouse, Tony and Steve caught each other up. Steve's team was closing in on Copperhead, who hadn't driven far from where Redwing had originally spotted him. They were surprised to hear about the development with Quantum-Freak joining their fight, but less surprised to hear about the Serpent Society's involvement. Tony promised to keep Cap and his team up to date on the details once he spoke to Quantum-Freak, and encouraged them to follow through on the plan to catch up with Copperhead in the meantime. The connection to the Serpent Society made it clear that Captain America's old nemesis was involved with Quantum-Freak's situation and possibly even the murder of Paulie Chase, and even if it didn't lead to any pertinent information regarding the Quantum-Freak situation, the idea of a soldier for the Serpent Society colluding with known mob members was worth investigating.

Tony ended the call just as the elevator arrived at the penthouse. He and Clint stepped out, and both found themselves stifling laughter at the sight of Thor sitting in awkward silence next to Quantum-Freak, literally twiddling his thumbs as she stared at her cell phone.

"Sorry to interrupt your riveting conversation," Tony said, "but we have some business to take care of here."

Quantum-Freak looked up, her eyes softening as they settled on Clint. "You good?"

He gave her a curt nod. "I'll be fine," he said, and then turned to Tony. "Any word on that coffee?"

Tony snapped his fingers twice, and a motorized catering cart wheeled smoothly into the room, complete with two pots of coffee, carafes of milk and cream, a bowl of sugar, four mugs, and a pile of mints. Thor grabbed a mug and began to shovel sugar into it, which earned him a side-eye from Anita, who filled her mug with black coffee. She did a double take when Clint grabbed the other pot and began to drink from it as if it were a cup.

"Is . . . that a thing that you normally do?" she asked.

"Well, this tastes about fifty-dollars per pound more expensive than the motor oil I buy," Clint said between slurps. "But coffee is coffee is coffee. Feeling better already."

"Hard core," she said, raising her mug.

"Check out this transition," Tony said, holding up both hands. "Speaking of hard core—huh, huh?—those are some incredible powers you have there. Now is about the time when you tell us exactly where Banner is being kept, what it is that you do, what the Serpent Society's plan is, and where you were going when we stopped you. We've got some ideas on all of them, but do yourself a favor and fill in the blanks for us before you outlast your usefulness."

Quantum-Freak sipped her coffee. "And you'll help me save my girlfriend's life."

"We shall," Thor said. Tony and Clint both nodded in agreement.

That seemed to be enough for Quantum-Freak. "All right, then. Warning you now, though. It's not much of an origin story."

"Doesn't have to be. Hawkeye's origin story is that he's very good at archery," Tony said. "And Thor? He's basically an exchange student."

"Iron Man got captured by terrorists," Clint chimed in. "He became a super hero by accident."

"Which actually *is* a cool origin story, but that's beside the point," Tony said, crossing his legs. "Continue."

"I don't know how they found me," Quantum-Freak said. "So much has happened, so it feels sort of like forever ago, but I guess it was . . . wow, just over a month. Carmella lost her job, so she was taken off her health insurance. She's always been really sick, since she was born. You saw it in her . . . her file or whatever. I don't know how much you know, but her mother . . . it doesn't matter, I guess. She barely got by on the medication her insurance provided, and it was all getting worse as it was. But without her job, we couldn't afford . . . I mean, even the basics. Medications she needs to breathe. You'd think that would be illegal, to withhold it. It's not. They can do anything they want. I posted online that

I was looking for work, any kind of work, and that's when they approached me."

"They who?" Tony asked.

"I didn't know at first," she said. "We met them at a coffee shop. Two guys and a lady. I actually haven't seen them since, so I don't know to what extent they were involved. Maybe just recruiting. I knew it was going to be something shady. Maybe trafficking. Carmella was scared, but I thought— whatever, you know? Whatever it is, I'll do it. The legal way had my girlfriend gasping for air every night. Racking up debt with emergency room visits we couldn't pay for. I figure, screw 'em."

She paused, and Tony noticed that her hands were shaking.

"You're scared to tell us," Tony said. "Scared that they'll come for you."

Quantum-Freak nodded.

Tony held her gaze. "Clint is alive because of you. Now, one might argue that Clint was also almost dead because of you, but I don't want to hear from 'one' right now. I want to help you. The other Avengers are already after the Serpent Society. You don't have anything to worry about."

Her reaction was not what Tony expected. She stood and began pacing, shaking her head. "Call them off. Seriously. Phononeutria almost took your whole team down, and she's just the start of this. The things they're creating in there . . .

you can't go in with half the team. You need everyone, all at once."

Thor furrowed his brow, letting out a chuckle. "This cannot be the same Serpent Society made up of those demented clowns who dress up like snakes? *They* are the ones who concern you?"

Quantum-Freak shook her head manically. "I don't know the Serpent Society you guys are talking about, but these people are serious. Dead serious. The muscle they have backing them up, it's . . ."

"I was under the impression that *you* were the muscle," Tony said. "You, your girlfriend, the other three. No offense, but there was a distinct lackey vibe you were giving off."

"That was part of the deal, yeah," she said, looking away from them. Tony could see in her eyes that she was ashamed, which he thought said a lot about her. "They've been creating these . . . I mean, I guess they're drugs, but they don't get you high. In exchange for helping them out, doing their dirty work, they gave me and Carmella a constant supply of injections. Just like that, Carm was fine. She could breathe. And she's still *there*. If they find out that I ratted them out, they might—"

"We'll get there. One thing at a time," Tony said.

"They gave you injections, too?" Clint asked. "Why?"

"That was part of the deal," she said. "The drugs didn't just heal her. They gave us our powers."

Stunned, Tony leaned in, narrowing his eyes. "Wait a second. You're telling me that you can rip open the fabric of reality because you got stuck with a needle?"

Quantum-Freak nodded. "And . . . gah, you know, I don't even want to say this. I haven't said this to Carmella. She knows I'm doing this for her, but—I know that what we were doing is wrong. I know that we're working for bad people. But when they told me the power I'd have, I've never been more excited in my life. I don't know what that says about my character, but there it is."

"The same is true of your formers allies, Phononeutria and the twins?" Thor asked. "Their powers come from this drug?"

"Yes," she said. "Please, though . . . understand, I'm not like Phononeutria. She's insane. Sadistic. The only reason I knew she could produce the antidote to her venom was because she attacked Deandre last week. Just for fun. Robbie mimicked her powers and produced the antidote himself. She would've let him die."

"So, Phononeutria aside, it seems like the Serpent Society cut you a pretty sweet deal," Tony said. "If you don't mind getting your hands dirty, that is. Why turn on them now?"

"Like I said, Carmella is in trouble," Quantum-Freak said. "Again. I don't know if it's the way the injection is responding to her disease, or if it's something else, but her power is supposed to come with complete regeneration. Every time she combusts, it takes longer for her to come back. After this last time, I didn't think she'd get up again. Ever. Black Mamba, she's the one in charge . . . she said she'd help, but she's just ignoring it. Every time, it gets worse. She's going to let Carmella die. I know it. And what's driving me insane is that, before the drug, she was dying . . . and now, the breathing problem is coming back and the drug itself seems to be killing her. I don't know what to do."

"Now," Tony said, "before we move on, I have many, many more questions. But I've held back asking about this, because Clint was the more immediate problem, and my good buddy Bruce is unkillable. And yet, I don't like the idea of not knowing where a close friend is. Can you help me out there?"

"He's alive," she said. "He's imprisoned in their laboratory. He's the one who told me you guys would help."

"A wise man," Thor said. "He was correct."

"Is that laboratory where you were headed when we caught you?" Tony asked. "Walk me through this, starting with the Barglewarf."

"Okay," Quantum-Freak said and, from the way her voice wavered, Tony knew that she was getting nervous. He needed as much information as possible, but he was aware that if he wanted her continued cooperation, he'd have to stop asking questions soon. It seemed that the more he dug in, the more nervous she got about turning on the Serpent Society. "They sent me and my group to Brooklyn, and told me to reach through the veil—that's just the partition between worlds, realities, space, time—and pull something nasty over from another world. Set it loose in the city. I don't know if it was to test my powers, or just to cause a distraction, but I was there all weekend trying. That's just one of a bunch of tests . . . they have me looking for all of these different worlds, realities, dimensions, seeing how far my powers can stretch."

"And it seems they stretch all the way to Asgard," Clint said.

"I guess. I just reached out for the strongest feeling, the most powerful signal, and I pulled. Finally, that thing came out—and then you did, too," she said, looking toward Thor. "I wonder if it was you that I felt to begin with."

"I am rather powerful," Thor said with a wide grin.

"Once that was done, we got word from the Serpent Society to head over to Long Island, to meet with this guy," she said. "Benny the Banger."

Clint hit Tony on the arm. "That's who Cap said was meeting with Copperhead, right?"

Tony nodded. "Clearly, you missed the Benny meeting, though. What was it going to be for?"

"It was a drop," she said. "That's all I know. Can you please help me save Carmella?"

"Like I said, one thing at a time," Tony said. "Now, all we need from you is two more things. One is easy, the other is decidedly less so. First . . . can you give us a location on the Serpent Society?"

"No. I don't know where they are."

"You said you've been in their facility before," Clint said. "I know you're worried about what they've got waiting for us, but trust me—we've been through the ringer. We've got this."

"That's not it," she said. "I really don't know. I've only ever gone there through portals. I just . . . it's hard to explain, but I feel a location, or a person, out . . . and then I can go there. Sometimes. It's weird. It works best when I have a fresh dose, and I haven't re-upped since yesterday morning, which in and of itself is making me twitchy."

"Gotcha. That brings me to the second thing," Tony said. "I've seen a lot in my time, Anita. I'm not a man who scares easily. But the idea of a drug that can give people the powers you and your crew have . . . that has me nervous. I'd love the chance to study this drug."

She looked at him, not catching on. "Okay?"

"Is there any chance that you can go back to the facility, get your re-up, and bring it back to me?"

Quantum-Freak looked at him as if he was crazy. "No way. I was specifically sent to kill you. I might not be the most, you know, morally sound person in the world, but I am *not* a good liar. If I went back there, they'd know immediately and I'd be dead. And besides, each injection is different. Specialized. I . . . I don't know the whole process, but

I'm telling you this because you have to be aware of what you're going into. It's not completely synthetic."

Tony uncrossed his legs, his mind working a million miles an hour. He already knew what she was going to say before she did, but he had to ask anyway. "What are they using to give you powers, Anita?"

Wringing her hands together, she looked away from the three of them. "I wouldn't have agreed to this if I knew. Not at first. I just wanted Carmella to survive. I found out when we were already deep into it . . ."

"Tell me," Tony said firmly, trying and failing to hide his frustration.

"The base of the drug is always the same, I guess. A mystical potion to make it all even stronger. But they're splicing it with blood from super humans they've kidnapped," she said. Then, her eyes shining, she looked at Tony, Clint, and Thor. "They have a laboratory full of people in there. That's how I got my powers. From another person."

CHAPTER TEN

SAVE THE PRINCESS

"Ah. Redwing sees him moving again," Falcon said, leaning toward the front of the Humvee, which was moving down the parkway in pursuit of Copperhead. "Uh . . . should I just say it out loud? Will it listen to me if I'm not Tony?"

"Yes, Mr. Wilson," F.R.I.D.A.Y.'s voice boomed over the speaker system before either Captain America or Black Widow could answer, a note of condescension in her voice. "You can just say it out loud. It will listen to you."

"Huh. Only Tony Stark would create an AI that sasses folks," Sam said. "Copperhead is back on the road, headed east down Sagtikos. And it looks like he has absolutely *no* regard for the speed limit. He's weaving in and out of traffic . . . and best part is, he's driving a mom car. Dummy."

"Let's pick up the speed, then," Cap chimed in. "He could lead us directly to the Serpent Society's hideout. Keep close, though—if we can catch him near the spot but before he goes inside, we could make him talk. Find out what he was doing meeting with Benny the Banger."

"You'd know the motivation better than the rest of us,"

Widow said, fiddling with her baton. With a flick of her wrist, it unlocked and doubled in length with a loud click. "What's the Serpent Society's usual MO?"

Cap felt his cell phone vibrate in his pocket. As he pulled it out, he sighed. "Their numbers aren't vast like Hydra. And their pockets don't run nearly as deep as the Maggia's. They operate in secret, working out of abandoned structures for the most part, only showing their faces when they have a new scheme. They're creatures of habit. You ever have a history teacher tell you that the most important part about studying past events is to learn where we went wrong, so that we don't repeat our mistakes?"

"Sure," Black Widow said.

"Well, the Serpent Society doesn't learn from their mistakes," Cap said, holding his cell phone in his hand. "They double down on them, trying the same types of schemes over and over, hoping that they'll someday hit pay dirt. They're unique among the threats I've faced in that they've never expanded . . . never truly grown into something formidable. And yet, at the same time, they just won't go away. We should be keeping an eye out for warehouses, hospitals, anything that has been shut down but not demolished. That's where they'll be." Cap held up his phone. "Hold on. Text from Tony."

Captain America's expression soured as he read the text. *Cap. Quantum-Freak says hold off on a confrontation. The*

Serpent Society has major muscle, big plans. We need the full team for this. Running a quick test here, and then we'll meet up. Figure out where these snakes are holed up.

"What is it?" Falcon asked. Next to him, Black Widow narrowed her eyes as she scanned her own cell phone, her face bathed in the light-blue glow.

"They want us to wait for them," Cap said, tapping out a quick text: *Copperhead is alone. We're all good here. Hurry.*

"What's the call, then?" Falcon said. "I can have Redwing keep an eye on him until everyone's on deck."

"I have redirected the drones to pursue Copperhead's vehicle from above as well," F.R.I.D.A.Y. said. "Coordinates have now been locked, and the car is tagged."

"We're not waiting," Cap said. "This is my call. I don't like the idea of holding off while Bruce is still unaccounted for. We're not launching a full infiltration; this is just one guy. One guy who I've wiped the floor with upward of ten times."

"Whoa," Black Widow said, squinting at her phone.

"Maybe ten is exaggerating," Cap admitted. "At least seven."

"No," Widow replied, shoving her phone toward Cap and Sam. They leaned toward it, and saw her screen open to a GPS map. "Look at this. You said the Serpent Society like to make themselves at home in abandoned warehouses, huh? How about an abandoned psychiatric hospital?"

Captain America watched on the screen as the pinpoint

that was their car moved toward the section of the map that Widow had zoomed in on. He clicked on the screen, and a little graphic came up: *Donald B. Halton Psychiatric Institution*, with the words CLOSED—PERMANENTLY in red text underneath.

"That's it," Cap said. "It looks like that's the only possible destination. Unless he turns around, that's the spot. This wouldn't even be the first time that the Serpent Society used an abandoned insane asylum. One was their base for years—they called it Serpent Citadel."

"Did you just say 'insane asylum'? Say this with me, Steve," Widow said, leaning in toward Captain America. "'Psychiatric hospital.' Psychiatric. Hospital."

"Sorry. Old habits. Psychiatric hospital," Cap complied. He looked over Widow and Sam's heads, raising his voice. "F.R.I.D.A.Y., can you confirm that Copperhead is en route to this location?"

"I was just about to, sir!"

"With the sass again," Falcon said, shaking his head. "So, it's basically a robotic, female Stark operating this car, huh?"

"Pretty much," Widow said.

"What's our ETA looking like?" Cap asked. "Can we catch up with Copperhead before he gets to the facility?"

"We will catch him in four minutes at our current rate," F.R.I.D.A.Y. replied. "Copperhead's vehicle has moved off the parkway."

Sam closed his eyes, communicating silently with Redwing. After a brief pause, he said, "And he's just straight up blowing red lights. I wouldn't be surprised if this dummy gets pulled over before we catch him."

"What's the deal? Could he somehow know that we're on his tail?" Cap asked.

"No way. Pretty sure he's just your typical road-rage scumbag, which makes me hate him twice as much," Sam said. "He's one of those guys that'll tailgate you in the slow lane when he could just move around you. Anyway, bad news is, he's gonna beat us there."

"Sam is correct," F.R.I.D.A.Y. said. "He will arrive at the facility approximately three minutes before us."

"What's the call, Cap?" Black Widow asked. "Do we wait? If we have the location already, we might as well play it safe."

Captain America put both hands on the bridge of his nose, weighing the options for a moment. If it was Hydra, he'd wait. If it was Count Nefaria's people, he'd wait.

"It's been a long night, and not a great morning," Cap said. "If we can get any pertinent information from Copperhead that'll help us end this sooner rather than later without alerting the rest of the Serpent Society, we should."

Falcon clapped his hands together. "That's what I want to hear. Because—I have to hand it to myself here—I just had a *great* idea."

"What is it?" Cap asked.

A sly grin spreading across his lips, Falcon closed his eyes. "Hey, Redwing," he said. "You see that big old rock, right off the road? Yeah. Grab that for me."

Captain America and Black Widow shot Sam quizzical looks, but he just kept on grinning.

"You'll see," he said as the Humvee pulled off the parkway and onto residential streets, closing in on the abandoned psychiatric hospital. "Oh, you'll see."

*　*　*

A lot of people thought that Tony Stark could do anything. While Tony was not one to shy away from the praise strangers liked to shower on him, that one bothered him a bit. Because it was just off from the truth.

Tony couldn't do anything. He could *learn* anything. Though some would argue that was a pedantic quibble, sometimes—like this very moment—it made all of the difference in the world.

While they waited for Tony's closest friend, Lieutenant Colonel James "Rhodey" Rhodes, also known as the Avenger War Machine, to arrive, Tony had taken a sample of Quantum-Freak's blood to run a series of diagnostics on in his workshop. Though he would've been able to get a quicker and more accurate analysis of the drug's properties if he had been able to run both the serum itself and

Anita's affected blood through the system, the advanced test program he was currently using would give him a 99.99999 percent accurate depiction of what the serum was doing to Quantum-Freak's body—perhaps then, by proxy, giving them an idea of what it might be doing to her girlfriend's. Tony wasn't as much of an expert on human and super-human biology as, say, Bruce Banner, but that's only because Banner was the best in the world.

But Tony was a close second. Considering he could replicate any organ with a functioning robotic implant in the time it took someone else to finish a crossword puzzle, Tony was rather comfortable being the runner-up in that field.

That was just the thing, he thought as he stared at the holographic projection of a bloodstream exposed to the Serpent Society's deadly concoction. He'd studied what he saw before him, and he'd learned . . . he knew exactly what the serum was doing to Anita. What he couldn't *do*, however, was be certain that he could reverse the damage.

F.R.I.D.A.Y. began to verbally explain what Tony was seeing, but he waved her off. "I programmed you to know this," he said. "I know this."

He stared at the holographic depiction of Anita's brain deteriorating on a loop. The brain tissue, flooded with the serum, was slowly being replaced by a glowing, pulsating putty that, oddly enough, continued to function like a brain . . . but *wasn't* made of organic, human tissue. Over and over, the 3-D projection went from a healthy brain to the shimmering substance that it was becoming as her body attempted—and failed—to fight the toxic agents in the serum. The glowing tissue snaked through her nervous system and all through her body, spreading and growing like a cancer—but not a cancer that interfered with her vital organs; she would still be able to function, and perfectly so.

It wasn't killing her. It was hollowing her out and filling her up with something else.

"Show me what happens if she detoxes now," Tony said. "If she stops today and we flush this garbage out of her system, does she bounce back?"

"Assessing." As F.R.I.D.A.Y. paused, Tony stood before the holographic system of organs and bones before him, watching again as it went from a functional person to a zombie. He didn't have to be Bruce Banner to know what the Serpent Society was doing. He looked away from the hologram as F.R.I.D.A.Y said, "Unable to determine with certainty. Most of her neural tissue remains unharmed—so far. It is difficult to conclude, using this blood sample, if the damage is self-perpetuating, or if the parasitic agent within the serum would die should the user stop administering the drug."

Tony's eyes settled on the lungs, as the glowing tissue spread through the hologram's chest. "A pair of healthy lungs could survive this parasite," Tony said aloud.

"That's not a question, Mr. Stark," F.R.I.D.A.Y. replied.

"Thinking aloud. Keep up," Tony said. "Unhealthy lungs ... the lungs of a smoker, maybe, or an asthmatic, someone with emphysema, with cystic fibrosis—this parasite would have a different effect, wouldn't it? The organ wouldn't be able to keep up."

"The numbing agent would lead to an initial boost in lung function, and the rest would be contingent on the super power used as a base of the serum. Certain powers would make unhealthy or damaged organs more resistant to any negative effects of the parasite," F.R.I.D.A.Y. said. "But—"

"But it wouldn't last. Figured. Good news," Tony said, his tone biting. He clenched his jaw. "Very good news, F.R.I.D.A.Y."

His AI knew Tony well enough to shut down the hologram and dim the lights in the workshop. Tony stood there, in the darkness, surrounded by his works in-progress, his inventions, his life, and wished that he could go up there and tell Anita that he'd put his mind to it and figured it out. But all he'd done was learn something.

What he would do with that knowledge, he had yet to decide.

* * *

In the penthouse of Stark Tower, Thor and Clint greeted Rhodes, who was already decked out in his War Machine armor. Much like a bulkier version of the Iron Man suit, but in dark-grey and black tones, Rhodey's armor was lined with heavy artillery that folded into the suit's back, which stored rocket launchers, machine guns, and enough firepower to light up the night. He was a walking weapon and, both because of his decorated military history and close friendship with Tony, there was no one the Avengers trusted more to handle the mantle of War Machine with dignity and care.

"You smell like athlete's foot," Rhodey said as Clint welcomed him into the room with a hug.

"Didn't you hear I almost died?" Clint said, pushing him toward Thor. "Give me a break! Let a dead man smell."

Rhodey, snickering, went to embrace Thor, but backed away. "Whoa! Are you kidding? What's going on here? Thor's over here reeking like a dumpster." He looked toward Quantum-Freak. "Let me guess, you reek, too?"

"Nope," she said. "Just them."

Clint and Thor looked at each other, and then back at Rhodey. At the same time, they said, "Barglewarf."

"You know what?" Rhodey said, shaking his head, "Not gonna ask."

Thor spread his arms wide, speaking in a hushed tone. "It was a grand battle over the streets of Bed-Stuy, which rang with screams of civilians below. They looked skyward as their mighty hero—me, that's me—emerged from the portal in the wake of the great, putrescent beast, and—"

"Heeeere we go," Rhodey said, turning toward Quantum-Freak as Thor continued, completely unaware that Rhodey had tuned out. "That's gonna go on for a long time. My name is Rhodey."

"I'm Quantum-Freak," she replied.

He shook her hand. "Isn't that a bit pejorative? Freak?"

She shrugged. "I'm hearing *your* name is War Machine. Isn't that a bit aggressive? Overcompensating, dude?"

Rhodey stared at her for a beat, and then turned to Clint. "Snappy, this one."

"Heed me!" Thor bellowed. "This is the best part. The puny Hawkeye knelt before his better, and begged, 'Oh, Mighty God of Thunder, may I fight alongside of you?' I replied, 'Of course, young man. Hold my cape as I slay this malodorous monstrosity.' And I—"

The *ding* of the elevator cut Thor off, as Tony Stark, donning his Iron Man armor, strode into the room.

"Good story," Iron Man said, clapping an exasperated Thor on the back.

"Wait a second, I'm still wondering what happened next in this creative interpretation of the time I saved the day without a lick of help from the Mighty God of Bragging Around Girls," Clint said, flicking a chip at Thor.

Thor snatched the chip out of the air with a sharp *crunch*.

Quantum-Freak rolled her eyes. "Gross. Taken, remember?"

"And we're about to go save her princess from the wicked dragon," Iron Man said. "Or serpent, as the case may be. It's all very romantic. Someone grab me a tissue. Feeling the tears coming on."

"I brag to everyone," Thor said with a shrug. "It is my way."

Anita stared at Tony, the trepidation plain on her face. "Did you find out anything? From the blood sample?"

Iron Man clasped hands with Rhodey, thanking him for coming, and then turned to Anita. "Yeah. I mean, there's still a lot to go through. It would help a great deal if we could get a sample of the serum. A few, even. But . . ."

"But?"

"But it's what I expected. It's more than just an injection that gives super powers. There's a catch, and it's not a fun one," he said, a hint of forced lightness to his tone, as if he was attempting to sound dismissive about the information. "I found a parasitic agent in your blood. From the quick analysis, I was able to break down its effects on a basic level, and it seems that . . . huh. Hard to explain. It eats your brain, and sure, okay, I know that sounds dramatic. It doesn't *eat* your brain."

Anita, Thor, Clint, and Rhodey gaped at him.

"I'm trying to figure out how to say this in a way that makes sense," Tony said. "It mystically produces new tissue that replaces the tissue of your brain. My thinking here—

and I'm going to go ahead and say that I'm right—is that the Serpent Society is using this parasitic agent to slowly replace your brain with an organ, created by said parasite, that will run your body in the same manner your brain does, only it will be completely programmable. Like a blank slate, waiting for a mystical command from a third party. Well, no, I'm not entirely sure if they'd control this tissue physically, magically, or if they'd surgically insert an implant that would feed directions to this new 'brain,'" he said, holding up two fingers on each hand and curling them as he said "brain." Then, he rolled his eyes. "Sorry for the quote fingers. That was lame. That was very substitute history teacher of me. Just trying to figure out how to say all this without it sounding . . . you know."

"Terrifying?" Quantum-Freak snapped. "Because, let me be the first to tell you, you're *not* doing well. Thoroughly terrified here."

"Well, I'm not here for bedside manner," Tony said. "I'm here to help you save Carmella and stop the Serpent Society from achieving whatever their end game is. If I'm scaring you, maybe that's okay. Maybe you should be scared."

"Tony," War Machine said.

Iron Man held up his hand, nodding. "Just saying. Just saying, is all."

"So it's turning me into a zombie," she said. "Ready to do their bidding."

"That's the working theory."

"Well, what about her, then?" Quantum-Freak asked. "If it's doing that to me, what is it doing to Carmella?"

"*Your* brain currently has minimal damage. Carmella's lungs, however . . . the effect of the parasite will cause massive internal scarring if we don't stop it. The fact that she can breathe right now is just an immediate, false cure. It will *not* help her in the long run. But we . . ." Tony said. He paused, holding Anita's gaze, a distant look in his eyes. Then, his expression growing stern, he inhaled sharply. "We're getting you off the serum. Today. Now. Same with Carmella. We'll stop this thing in its tracks."

Quantum-Freak stared at him. "Are you telling the truth?"

Tony clenched his jaw, his eyes darting to the side and then back to Anita. "Yeah. I am. You and your girlfriend are going to be fine."

She let out a little laugh, and then covered her mouth. "Sorry. Hah. I know that's the craziest reaction someone has ever had to being told they have brain damage," she said. "But . . . wow. You really are going to help me."

Tony nodded. His helmet snapped shut, covering his face as, before him, a smile crept over Anita's lips for the first time since they'd met.

"You said you can only get to a place by *feeling* it," Tony said. "Does that mean that, when you open this portal, we're gonna be smack dab in the middle of their lair?"

"Yeah," she said. "Or . . . I could take you to Captain America."

"That one," Clint said. "Let's do that one."

Iron Man turned around, clapping his hands together. "All right, everyone. We're doing this. Avengers vs. the Serpent Society. Quantum-Freak, let's see you do your freaky thing. That came out wrong. Make a portal. And F.R.I.D.A.Y., let Cap's team know we're on the way."

As Anita waved her hands, opening up a crackling, red portal in the middle of the room, Tony caught War Machine looking at him from his open face mask—and it was clear that he saw right through him.

Tony shook his head. "Don't say a word."

War Machine let out a deep sigh. "Oh, man."

"Yeah." Tony looked his friend in the eye for a moment and then turned toward the portal. "Avengers assemble," he said halfheartedly, and stepped through the rift.

CHAPTER ELEVEN

FOR NOW

Copperhead was sloppily singing along to an oldies but goodies station when a rock the size of a bowling ball crashed through his windshield and landed right in his lap, sending a shower of broken glass raining down over the dashboard and his legs. The pain sank deep into his gut, causing him to jerk to the side, his hands still grasping the wheel. The car veered off the road and slammed up over the curb, onto an open stretch of grass.

The car jerked violently as Copperhead drove it over the field, the wind whipping at his face through the hole in the windshield. He hit the brakes, chunks of glass sliding off his lap and to the car's floor as he came to a stop. He put the car in park and slowly, tenderly, lifted the jagged rock off of his lap, groaning loudly.

He stumbled out of the car and looked up at the sky, silently wondering if he'd just been hit by a comet. If anyone had been passing by this deserted road, he would've been a strange sight indeed, even if he hadn't been clutching his gut in pain, standing in front of a car with a boulder-shaped hole in its windshield, looking up at the sky as if searching for UFOs.

Copperhead, much like many of the other members of the Serpent Society, took the symbology of their organization rather seriously. While Black Mamba, who had earned the role of leader in the past year, settled for wearing a serpent pin in her hair, Copperhead took it quite a bit further. He wore a copper suit of scale mail, which included a tunic, gloves, and, most notably, a headpiece that looked quite like the snake from which he took his name had wrapped itself around his head and had begun to swallow him.

Copperhead squinted at the sky, his lips curled up in a sneer. "You're *kiddin'* me," he said aloud, as he saw what he believed to be yet another "comet" descending from above. Realizing that it was going to hit him right where he stood, he darted toward his car, looking over his shoulder as he scrambled to get in. The object shooting toward him changed directions, following him as he moved.

He grimaced. "Huh?"

At the moment that the Falcon, his crimson wings spread wide, came into sight, it was too late for Copperhead to move. Falcon thrust his legs forward, delivering a powerful kick to Copperhead's chest, sending him slamming into his car. The force of the blow shattered the driver-side window.

Copperhead, grunting in fury, pushed away from the

car as the Falcon landed gracefully on the grass. Before Copperhead could get to his feet, a Humvee pulled up and came to a stop behind the Falcon. Captain America and Black Widow hopped out of the back while Copperhead's mind raced, trying to think of the best course of action before it was too late. He *really* wanted to kill them, but, historically, that hadn't worked out in his favor. He was so close to the Society's hideout—another quarter mile of driving and he would have been at the gates to the abandoned parking lot. If he could alert Black Mamba somehow and get their goons out here, there was no way these three would stand a chance. Especially not with the latest addition to their collection of serums. It would be over in an instant.

"Thinking you can make a dash for it?" Falcon said. "I'd like to see you try. I'm willing to bet you're not so fast now that you're out of that rust bucket you call a car."

Copperhead shot a glance over his shoulder, and then turned back to the three Avengers, sneering. He knew the Falcon was right.

"Guess it's a fight, then," he said. He held out his gauntlets, equipped with poison blasts—which were actually not poisonous at all, but were in fact electrical discharges that hit his enemies with a series of debilitating shocks. The name may not have been accurate, but he had to maintain the snake theme at all costs.

Captain America and Black Widow moved toward Copperhead, who assumed a defensive stance, but Falcon held up his hands, stopping them from charging. In the sky above him, Redwing punctuated the movement with an echoing cry.

"Allow me," Falcon said. "I think I earned this one."

Cap grinned, inclining his head. "I can't say I wouldn't love to see this. Make me proud."

"You know I will," Falcon said, turning back toward Copperhead. Falcon strode toward him, cracking his knuckles. "So, what's it gonna be? Feeling like a villain monologue? I'd love to hear what you guys are up to. Could be good for a laugh."

Copperhead sneered at him. "We *want* you to laugh at us. That way, when it's too late, you'll have that moment of perfect shock . . . and then, as you die, you will see the truth of what we have done."

Falcon stopped a yard away from him. "You're a grown man dressed like a snake. I'm all *types* of not afraid of you."

"It's not me you should be afraid of," Copperhead said. "It's *us*."

"Somehow, still not scared," Falcon said, lunging at Copperhead.

Anticipating the move, Copperhead leaned in to Falcon, shooting a poison blast from his hand—but Falcon's punch had been a fake out. He'd launched himself into the air behind

Copperhead, and landed a cracking punch to the back of the headpiece, sending Copperhead stumbling forward. Falcon followed through with kick to the small of his back, but Copperhead's armor absorbed the brunt of the blow.

Falcon backed up as Copperhead got to his feet. Copperhead balled his fists together and swung at Falcon, who dodged the blow. They traded punches, with Falcon nimbly avoiding each of Copperhead's crosses and jabs, clearly toying with him—until Copperhead thrust his head forward, slamming the top of his headpiece into the bridge of Falcon's nose.

Falcon stumbled backward, and Copperhead used the opportunity to lean in and trigger one of his copper bursts right in the winged Avenger's face. The copper burst—a flash bomb that blasted out of the snake's mouth on his headpiece—was blinding for all except Copperhead, whose special lenses protected his eyes from its effects.

Falcon looked up at him from the ground, seemingly blinded from the effects of the burst. Copperhead lifted his steel boot, preparing to stomp on the fallen hero's neck. He *could've* taken the opportunity to make a break for it, because both Captain America and Black Widow were still shielding their eyes in the background, rendered sightless by the blast.

But no. Copperhead had just beaten an Avenger. If he didn't take the Falcon's life, right here and now, he'd always regret it. Showing the world that the Serpent Society was not to be overlooked was part of their whole thing, anyway—and

Copperhead knew he would rise to the top of the chain of command if he walked into Black Mamba's office and threw the Falcon's wings onto her table.

He brought his foot down toward Falcon's neck, but his leg locked, stopping short. Looking down, he saw Falcon's hands grasping his foot, one at the front, and one at the ankle. Falcon grinned.

Then, the winged Avenger pulled his hands in opposite directions, twisting Copperhead's foot with a painful *snap*. Indescribable pain shot up his ankle and Copperhead dropped, watching in awe as Sam, completely unimpeded by the copper burst, stood over him.

"These, right here?" Falcon said, tapping on his dark goggles. "These aren't just to look cool."

Pinning Copperhead to the ground with his knee, the Falcon ripped off the villain's gauntlets as well as the headpiece, removing all of his means of attack as Captain America and Black Widow strode over to him, wiping their eyes. Copperhead didn't resist this time. He might have been a murderer and a terrorist who dressed like a reptile, but he was self-aware enough to know when he was beaten.

Cap knelt down beside Copperhead, his face grim, his voice forceful. "What's the plan?"

"You'll know soon enough," Copperhead said, letting out a hissing laugh despite the static bursts of pain shooting up his ankle and shin.

"You'd be smart to start talking," Cap said. "How do the injections factor in?"

"Figure it out," Copperhead said.

"Figure *this* out," Black Widow said. "You're already losing. We have your kids in S.H.I.E.L.D. custody. We know where your lair is. We know where the Hulk is. And from the sound of what Falcon just did to you, you're coming up short one ankle. If I were you, I'd start making my case. Because this is looking worse and worse for you and your buddies."

"You were meeting with Benny the Banger," Cap said. "Why?"

"Why don't you ask *him*?" Copperhead said. "He may be a disloyal *rat*, but not me."

Black Widow and Captain America shared a look. Cap turned back to Copperhead and began patting him down.

"Hey! Come on!" Copperhead shouted.

Cap reached into Copperhead's belt and withdrew a vial of red liquid that had shattered during the fight. With the shards of glass, dipped in liquid red, in his hand, Cap didn't have to wonder what the substance was for long. The coppery smell filled his nostrils.

"It's blood," he said, his mind already piecing together the clues. "Is the Maggia supplying you with super-human blood?"

"Wouldn't you like to know?" Copperhead snapped.

Captain America discarded the shards of glass and wiped

his glove off. "One more chance. Your facility is about to get overrun by the Avengers, in full force. You're headed toward a lengthy prison sentence, courtesy of S.H.I.E.L.D. Whatever you're trying to do here, it's *not* working. Your plan failed. Again."

Copperhead looked up at them with bleary eyes, his expression souring. Deflated, he shook his head. "It wasn't my plan. Maybe if they *did* listen to my plan from the start. . . . The Serpent Society has *never* trusted outsiders! I told them this would be their downfall."

"So bringing in the kids, you didn't want that?" Captain America said. "What was *your* plan?"

Copperhead breathed in deeply, thinking back to two months earlier, when the Serpent Society had first set up in their new lair . . .

* * *

Black Mamba had sat at the head of their new conference room, with the rest of the currently active Serpent Society behind her. Together, they had just concocted their plan for what would be their biggest assault on the United States of America under Black Mamba's recently established leadership. Copperhead, however, was more of a classicist than her, and just before they adjourned, he had insisted they give him the floor. He had, he'd promised, a better plan. A plan that would truly set the newly reformed Serpent Society apart from the failures of their previous attempts at grasping true power.

Copperhead had cleared his throat, his hands folded behind his back as he stood before the Serpent Society.

"Now that we have the technology," Copperhead had said, slowly, dramatically, "we must think *bigger* than we have been. Forget recruitment. Forget building an army. We must make a statement!"

"Go on," Black Mamba had said, her voice dripping with contempt.

"We will create a mutation agent, powerful and swift, and we will release it in Manhattan's water supply," Copperhead had said, relishing his affected pause. "And it will turn the entire population of New York City . . . into snakes!"

Everyone in the room had stared at him, dumbfounded. His arms spread, his eyes darted from comrade to comrade, awaiting a reaction. After a tense, prolonged moment of silence, Copperhead lowered his hands, shifting awkwardly, and Black Mamba turned to the rest of the Serpent Society.

"So," she had said, rolling her eyes. "About that *serum*."

* * *

The Falcon snapped his fingers in front of Copperhead's distant gaze. The villain started back to the here and now, staring up at Cap, the Falcon, and Black Widow.

"You know what?" Copperhead said, his face twisting. He stared at Captain America with abject hatred. "Forget it. No one appreciates an out-of-the-box idea. It's always hire the muscle, bomb the . . ."

He trailed off, as the three Avengers leaned in, waiting for him to finish.

"Bomb?" Cap said, grabbing him by the scale mail. "Bomb *what*?"

"It was just an example!" Copperhead said, twisting in Captain America's grasp. "Do what you want to me. No matter what's happening now, in the long game, the Serpent Society will *not* lose. No matter how many goons get locked up, that doesn't matter. That's just static. The strength of the Society itself will continue to grow. Defeat us now and we will rise again, stronger and nastier each time. So maybe back down while you still can."

Cap spun Copperhead around so his stomach was against the grass and pulled a wire out of his own utility belt. He wrapped it around Copperhead's hands, binding them behind his back and pulling the cord extra tight. He ushered the limping villain to the back of the Humvee, where he'd stay until they were done with their infiltration.

Sam pointed in the direction of the psychiatric hospital's gate.

"Whoa," he said, pulling off his goggles. "Are you seeing this?"

A spot of red energy appeared in midair and then, with a surge of power, the energy shot out, ripping a big hole in the sky. Sam bent down, preparing to attack whatever came out, but Black Widow casually held out her baton, stopping him.

"Nuh-uh," she said. "That's Iron Man. He said he'd be coming with Quantum-Freak . . . part of me, for some reason, pictured a vehicle involved."

Thor, Hawkeye, Iron Man, War Machine, and Quantum-Freak emerged from the portal, one after the other, with the ease of a group of people walking through a door. Most of them, anyway. War Machine kept casting uneasy glances over his shoulder, as if he expected to see a monster following him from the darkness of the portal.

"Hey, Rhodes," Black Widow said. "You good?"

"Yeah," Rhodey said as she patted him on the shoulder. "Just not used to walking through a dimensional rift. Makes a man ask some existential questions. That's all."

Falcon looked Quantum-Freak up and down over his glasses. "You made that? The portal?"

"It's what I do," she said. Then, she let out a defeated snicker. "For now."

"Well, then. Welcome to the team," Falcon replied, shaking her hand. "For now."

Iron Man looked at the abandoned Donald B. Halton Psychiatric Institution in the distance beyond the gate. It wasn't close enough for the Serpent Society to have seen both the throwdown with Copperhead and Quantum-Freak's portal, but not far enough away to be sure they were safe from surveillance. They may have lost the element of surprise, but at least they had the full team. The building wasn't dilapidated, but the dark windows and the empty parking lot around it made it look vacant, like a tombstone looming over them from afar.

"That's it, huh?" he said.

"Like I said, I feel out a location," Anita said. "I've been back and forth to this one through the rift more than any other place. That's it. I've never seen it from outside, though. I think . . ." She closed her eyes and held her hand low to the ground, red energy pulsing between her fingertips. "I think they're underground. Carmella's room is cut from concrete, so she doesn't . . . you know, explode the whole building if she has a bad dream. I just don't know how *far* underground."

Iron Man nodded. "Yeah, they're underneath the building, operating out of the lower levels. We've got a small tunnel cutting through the building's foundation, which is where I'm gonna guess they're keeping your girl. Which, from where I'm standing? Not safe."

Clint arched a brow. "You two psychic now? What's going on?"

"My HUD has a 3-D scan of the building's layout," Iron Man said. "Looking at it right now. Also, when Rhodey and

I took out Count Nefaria's new spot last month, we found that he built an entire multi-level structure under a little shack in the woods. This isn't nearly that, but it's almost more unsettling. Operating in the public like this—no matter if the building is abandoned—it's bold. They have to be planning something big."

"Copperhead let it slip that there's a bomb," Black Widow said. "He played it off, though. Wouldn't elaborate."

"A bomb," Thor questioned, looking toward Anita, "or a person who acts as one?"

"You think they could be planning to force Carmella to detonate somewhere?" Cap asked. "Hurt people?"

Quantum-Freak's eyes widened in panic. "I—I don't know. They never said that, but . . ."

"But why else give her that power?" Tony finished for her.

"That's something we'll have to find out. But for now, let's focus on the task at hand," Cap said. "Anita says we need all hands on deck. I'm choosing to believe her. We're launching a full assault, now. Iron Man, Thor, Falcon, War Machine—you four take to the skies as we approach, keeping an eye out for any attackers from the upper levels of the building. When we approach the front entrance, come back to the group. I want to breach the entrance strong, as a single unit. Tony, can you give me a head count?"

"My HUD shows no shortage of warm bodies in there. They're spread out through the building. F.R.I.D.A.Y. counts thirty-two, but they're in the tunnel area that I can't get a read on," Iron Man said. "If a good amount of them are juicing up on this serum, we could run into a problem."

"Anita, you know some of these people," Cap said. "And *I* know the Serpent Society. Here's what we do. When we engage an enemy, shout out what you know about them. What power they have, whatever you can tell us that'll be helpful. I'll do the same for the Serpent Society soldiers I know. We want to make this quick, surgical. The goal is to rescue Bruce Banner and Carmella, to retrieve a sample of their serum and destroy the rest, and to—if possible— detain Black Mamba. The other Serpent Society members, engage them, drop them, move on. Mamba is making the power move here, so she's the one we aim for. Understood?"

"Understood," the other Avengers echoed. Quantum-Freak looked at them, unsure what to say, so nervously echoed the word seconds later. Thor offered her an encouraging grin.

The flyers took off into the sky, as Captain America led Black Widow, Hawkeye, and Quantum-Freak on foot toward the Serpent Society's secret lair.

As they jogged, keeping to the side of the road to stay as clear from the building's view as possible, Captain America let Clint and Natasha get ahead of him, and fell in pace with Quantum-Freak.

"My understanding is that you did all this to save your

girlfriend," he said. "I don't know if I'd call what you did noble, but I would call it understandable. Human."

Quantum-Freak looked at Cap, narrowing her eyes at him. "You don't have to call it noble. I'd do it again."

"And I can't fault you for it," Cap said. "S.H.I.E.L.D. might. But we'll cross that bridge when we come to it. How about the others?"

"What others?"

"Phononeutria. Robbie, Deandre," he said. "You wanted to give Carmella a way to survive—and, let's be honest, you wanted to hit back at the government for the situation they put you in."

"You wouldn't understand," Quantum-Freak said.

"People think that about me a lot," Captain America said. "They see the red, white, and blue, they hear the name . . . they think I'm a relic. This guy who salutes the flag while closing his eyes, turning his back to everyone this country leaves behind. And I do believe in this country. I believe that it can be better, and that we have to fight to make it so. If this place was perfect and if people weren't getting hurt, I wouldn't have to wear the Stars and Stripes anymore."

Quantum-Freak looked at him, her expression softening. "Robbie and Deandre . . . I don't know them that well. They were nice, though. Are nice. I'm probably never going to see them again," she said. "They both—and I don't know too much about it, but Deandre told me one night. Robbie never spoke about it. They both have a rare blood disease. Their twin—I guess, their triplet . . . he died from it. They came looking for the same thing Carmella and I were. Help."

"In exchange for your services," Captain America said.

"Yeah," Quantum-Freak said. Then, softly, she added, "Why not?"

"And Phononeutria?"

Quantum-Freak shook her head. "I don't know if anything was wrong with her. Physically," she said. "Besides, you know, she's a psycho."

"I did pick that up," Cap said. As they closed in on the facility, he turned to Anita, preparing to say something that he never got to finish.

At once, from above, Iron Man, Thor, War Machine, and Falcon shouted a warning that was quickly drowned out by the screaming sound of a missile rocketing toward them from the open door of the Serpent Society's hideout.

CHAPTER TWELVE

RIFTS

The missile whistled toward Captain America, propelled forward by an intense shower of glowing sparks flying out from its base. The Avengers acted at once. Black Widow and Hawkeye dove to the side, while Captain America raised his shield with his right hand, reaching out with his left to hold Quantum-Freak behind him. From above, the airborne Avengers cracked into defensive action. Thor and Falcon flew over to the open door of the facility in pursuit of the attacker, who remained hidden in the darkness of the building. Iron Man sent a beam of repulsor power at the incoming projectile while War Machine fired three miniature guided missiles, but the missile was already too close to Cap—it was going to hit its target.

Cap braced for the explosion, and then, right before the missile would've collided with the Vibranium shield, the sky ripped open with a thunderous crack.

Silence followed.

Peering around his shield, Cap watched in amazement as the air before him surged with red energy, and then, with a loud sucking sound, closed in on itself, swallowing the missile whole.

Behind Captain America, Quantum-Freak stood, her knees buckled, a trickle of sweat pouring down her temple, red energy dissipating from her hands.

She looked at Cap, offering a pained smile. Cap nodded in approval. "Good move."

"We're gonna need a lot more than that," she said, turning back to the building. Cap followed her gaze to watch as Thor and Falcon were met at the door by a battalion of armed Serpent Society soldiers—some of them clad in snake-themed costumes, others looking much like Quantum-Freak and her team had . . . just a group of kids that could've been coming from a college class. But here they were, their bodies poisoned by power that wasn't theirs, ready to fight to the end of the line for what the Serpent Society had offered them.

"Here we go!" Cap said, running toward the incoming parade of villains. "Iron Man, what are we dealing with?"

"Fourteen on the ground! One with a bazooka!" Iron Man said, launching toward the incoming group of Serpent Society members and their lackeys. A leather-clad man, sickly and bald but with glowing, green eyes, held a rocket launcher aimed at the Avengers. He let out another missile with a deafening blast, which, this time, Thor intercepted with a pointed toss of Mjolnir.

The projectile exploded in the sky as Thor flew toward

the shooter, landing in front of him the moment that his hammer arced back to him. Its handle met Thor's palm just in time for him to slam Mjolnir into the rocket launcher itself, sending it flying out of the shooter's grasp.

"Good work, Thor!" Cap called out as he raced across the parking lot.

"Watch out!" Quantum-Freak cried as Thor closed in on the shooter. "That's Volcano Breath! He can—"

The shooter smirked and then opened his mouth. A stream of golden energy shot out from his throat, blasting Thor in the chest. The mighty God of Thunder was lifted into the air and sent flying across the parking lot.

"He can do that," Quantum-Freak finished sheepishly.

Captain America let his shield fly, hitting Volcano Breath in the back of the head. As the shield arced back to Cap, Volcano Breath fell, crumbled on the ground. All around him, skirmishes between the other Avengers and their opposition had broken out. The closest of them was still yards away from the entrance to the mental facility, fighting on the pavement of the otherwise deserted parking lot.

Cap ducked a swipe from a spandex-clad woman, whom he recognized as Fer-de-Lance, a longtime member of the Serpent Society. She had twin eight-inch blades that extended from her forearm sheaths, turning both of her fists into deadly claws.

Catching another blow from her claws on his shield, Cap

scanned the field. He kicked Fer-de-Lance in the sternum, but she was prepared, scooting back to lessen the force of the blow.

"I think I'm seeing a few I recognize!" Cap shouted. "I think the rest are on the serum. Gotta get closer to tell!"

He grabbed Fer-de-Lance's arm as she attempted to stab him in the throat, using the force of her attack to send her flying over his shoulder.

"I've got Fer-de-Lance over here," Cap said as she hit the ground. "Enhanced strength, durability. Nothing I can't handle."

She sprang up, reeling back her fist to swipe at Cap again. Cap anticipated it with a sweeping kick to her legs. This time, as she fell, he caught her with a blow to the spine with his balled fist, and then slammed her into the ground. He glanced up to see Iron Man fighting a green and blue-clad villain who had taken Copperhead's costume design a bit further. His headpiece was the large, green head of a snake, with his eyes and nose peering from the mask's open mouth. Iron Man, floating ten feet above ground, launched a flurry of repulsor blasts at him, which the villain dodged. The pavement turned to rubble with each blow, but the villain remained unscathed. With every move Iron Man's opponent made, he began to expand, growing taller and bulkier, until he had reached a height of ten feet.

He caught Iron Man's foot and flung him to the ground,

letting out a deep, booming laugh as the shocked golden Avenger bounced along the grass.

"Iron Man—that's Puff Adder! Super strength, toxic gas, and—" Captain America's warning was cut short as Fer-de-Lance leapt up and landed a deep scratch to his side. He brought his elbow down, catching her arm between his ribs, and then swung his arm to the side, cracking her in the chin. She fell to the ground, unconscious, and Cap leapt away from her, heading toward Hawkeye, who was launching a series of electrically charged arrows at a bulky, bearded man in ripped jeans, who didn't seem to mind the voltage he was being pumped with.

"Let me guess," Iron Man said, flying up to get out of Puff Adder's powerful grasp. "He gets insanely big!"

"Only lasts fifteen minutes," Cap said, as he flung his shield toward the hulking man who was now throwing the sparking arrows back at Hawkeye.

"Won't need that long," Iron Man said, zipping around Puff Adder, who leapt madly at him, trying to snatch him out of the sky.

Cap's shield hit the bulky man's skull with a ringing blow. As Cap ran to catch the shield, he was stunned to see the man shoot him a withering look, not so much as a red mark on his skin.

The man tilted his head to the side. "*Really?*"

Hawkeye joined Cap's side as he prepared to go head to

head with their foe. "Now you see what I'm dealing with."

"Anita!" Cap called out. "Who is this?"

Quantum-Freak, ducking as Falcon threw one of the lackeys toward the ground, ran toward Cap and Hawkeye to get a better look. She squinted as they both went blow for blow with the bearded man.

"Watch out, that's Mr. Unbreakable!" she cried.

Cap dodged a punch from Unbreakable, who, true to his name, didn't have a single blemish on his skin regardless of how many times Cap and Hawkeye struck him. Unbreakable followed through with another punch, and Cap grabbed his arm, pulling him in to strike him with a head-butt.

"I know whose powers you stole," Cap said, jumping back in line next to Hawkeye. "Luke—"

Unbreakable threw himself forward, returning Cap's head-butt, and then swinging his head at Hawkeye, too. "These are MY powers!"

As Cap and Hawkeye battled Unbreakable, Cap glanced across the parking lot to check in on the rest of the Avengers. Iron Man landed a beam of repulsor power in Puff Adder's face, sending him stumbling back into a crew of lackeys that Thor and War Machine were handling, back to back.

"Good looking out," War Machine said, ducking a punch from a woman with scales sprouting up on her body. Her eyes began to glow and she whipped her spiked tail at him. Rhodey successfully evaded the attack, allowing Thor to catch it. Tail in one hand, hammer in the other, he swung the reptilian woman at Puff Adder, and then followed through with a crushing blow from Mjolnir, which caused the engorged villain to deflate back to his normal size. He discarded the scaled woman off to the side and flipped his hammer in his hand.

"Amateurs," Thor said.

Cap and Hawkeye, trading blows with Unbreakable, who didn't seem to show any sign of slowing down, backed toward the rest of the group. All around, the Avengers continued to fight with the Serpent Society's thugs, taking them out one by one. Cap threw a glance over his shoulder toward Black Widow and Quantum-Freak, who were locked in battle with another green-clad Serpent Society goon.

"That's King Cobra!" Cap shouted, slamming his shield repeatedly into Unbreakable's face, as Hawkeye upped the ante, loading explosive arrows into his bow. Cap jumped back from his attacker and covered his face with his shield as Clint launched the arrows, which exploded on impact. "His bones don't break, his muscles can't tear—he has full control over the size and shape of his body. Do *not* let him grab you!"

King Cobra looked to be the most vicious foe so far. He wore a hood that flared out, like the head of his namesake, and his glowing yellow eyes flashed as he lashed out at Black Widow and Quantum-Freak.

"Too late!" Black Widow cried, as King Cobra snatched

her wrist. His arm bent around hers, wrapping around her forearm like a snake. She jabbed her wrist into his neck and triggered her bracelet. Electrostatic-energy blasts fired into him with a series of cracks, delivering thirty thousand volts to his body. He convulsed and his glowing eyes rolled back into his head, but he didn't let go. His grip tightened, and he pulled her in.

Quantum-Freak began to open up a portal below him, but Black Widow shouted, "No! He'll pull me right in! Help, Cap!"

Captain America opened his mouth to reject her order, but Quantum-Freak was too fast.

She whirled her hand around in the air and the portal followed suit, like a lasso. It shot toward Cap and Hawkeye, just as Unbreakable was launching another series of crushing punches at them. He didn't even have time to look up before the portal enveloped him and then closed with him in it.

And Captain America couldn't complain about that.

He raced toward Black Widow, who, still in King Cobra's grasp, had whipped out her baton. She lifted it high above King Cobra's face, preparing to crack him with it until he loosened his grip. Right before she brought it down on him, and before Cap could get to her side, a blur of red and brown shot into his face.

Redwing, his wings spreading, dug his talons into King Cobra's eyes. King Cobra screamed in agony, bringing both hands to his face, letting Black Widow go. Falcon landed between Widow and King Cobra, grinning as he watched his loyal winged friend claw at the villain's face.

"Thanks," Widow said.

"Eh, you would've gotten him," Falcon said, spreading his wings as he charged King Cobra. "Redwing just couldn't stand to sit this one out."

Black Widow smiled at him, and then turned to Quantum-Freak. "Good job," she said as Cap and Hawkeye jogged over. The ranks of the Serpent Society and their lackeys were severely lessened, with Thor and Iron Man finishing off the final group closer to the building.

"You didn't, uh . . . send that Unbreakable guy to hell, did you?" Hawkeye asked. Cap had been wondering the same thing.

"No," Quantum-Freak said. "The first thing I could think of was the garbage dump, so . . . I guess he's smellier than you now."

"Hah!" Clint said. "This one. She's something."

"We have to keep track of these people," Cap said. "S.H.I.E.L.D. has to know where to pick them up so we can flush the serum from their systems."

"Oh," Clint said. "Right. Still. The garbage dump is pretty funny."

"We should rethink the plan. They're clearly trying to keep us outside of the building," Black Widow said. "Cap . . . if the team stays outside and they focus on keeping us out, they might not expect an attack from within."

"What are you thinking?" Cap asked.

Black Widow turned to Quantum-Freak. "Can you open a portal and get us inside, to Carmella and Bruce? Once we find them, we can get you and your girlfriend out of here so we can *end* this."

Quantum-Freak nodded, but her eyes were wild. "Yes. I think." She waved her fingers, which sparked with red power, but the solid bolt of electricity that once danced across her palms were gone.

"Your powers," Captain America said. "What's happening?"

Quantum-Freak breathed in slowly, and then gritted her teeth, waving her hands in a circle. The air rippled with bursts of red power, and then opened in a wavering portal, smaller and weaker than before.

"They're not my powers," Quantum-Freak said. "The serum is wearing off."

Black Widow looked at her with a solemn expression. "Well, then. Let's hurry."

Together, as the rest of the Avengers continued to clash with the Serpent Society and their serum-empowered cronies in the parking lot, Black Widow and Quantum-Freak leapt through the rift in the sky.

Captain America, with Hawkeye by his side, ran over to the rest of the Avengers just as the last enemy standing—a young woman whose skin glowed like the aurora borealis—looked at the incoming group of heroes and ran across the parking lot, heading for the road. War Machine started after her, but Iron Man grabbed his arm.

"Nah, let her go," Iron Man said, holding out his gauntlet. His wrist opened up and a drone the size of a fly popped out and followed the young woman. "I don't know if most of these kids knew what they were getting into. The drone will let us know where she goes when it's time for S.H.I.E.L.D. to pick her up."

"A poor excuse," Thor said. "The choices we make define us. We are nothing if not a collection of stories we have told throughout our lives."

"I thought you liked Quantum-Freak," Hawkeye said.

"Aye," Thor said, shrugging. "I suppose I am forgiving in nature. My brother is Loki, after all."

Falcon, War Machine, Thor, Iron Man, and Hawkeye gathered around Cap, who pointed at the door. "Black Widow and Quantum-Freak are going to pop inside, attempt to rescue Carmella and Banner, and then pop right back out. We have to keep them fighting."

"Storm the castle, then," Iron Man said. "This kinda thing never gets old."

"We have to . . ." Cap started, but then trailed off, furrowing his brow.

"We have to what?" Hawkeye asked.

"Do you hear that sound?" Cap said, narrowing his eyes. By the time he'd finished the question, the ground began to shake beneath them. The Avengers stepped into formation around him, facing the mental facility, silently answering Cap's question.

The double doors burst off their hinges as a monster the size of the Humvee barreled through the entrance, running toward them with earth-shaking bounds. He was once a human, but his muscles were engorged, his veins bursting with each flex, his bones elongated and jutting out of his limbs like blades. He roared as he ran toward them, beating his green fists on his enormous chest.

"The serum," Cap said, his voice hushed with panic as they braced for a fight. "They made a Hulk."

* * *

Black Widow stepped out of the portal and into the dark, dank, reinforced cell, its rocky walls scorched from what must have been endless fits of spontaneous combustion. Carmella, deep bags ringed around her dark eyes, looked up at her from the corner, where she sat on the floor taking in long, gasping breaths. A moment later, as the red glow of the portal shifted, Carmella looked past Black Widow, relief flooding her gaunt face.

"Anita!" she gasped, a pained sound.

Anita rushed past Black Widow as the portal closed behind her and threw her arms around her girlfriend. She held her there, on the floor, cradling Carmella's head against her face as Black Widow gazed around the room. It was a prison, not even fit for an animal. She could scarcely believe that Anita and Carmella had been driven to choose this life, though she knew that any room that was approaching comfortable wouldn't have been able to withstand a detonation from Carmella. Seeing them there, sobbing as they embraced each other, removed any remaining reservations that she had about Anita's intentions. She really wanted nothing more than to save Carmella, and it made Black Widow's blood boil that the Serpent Society had used her desperation as a weapon. Widow had been used by people who had done the same thing to her, and she knew that there was only one way to deal with those kinds of people.

Show them no mercy.

Anita helped a trembling Carmella to her feet, keeping her arm around her waist. "Come on. It's going to be okay. We just have to get to the lab before they find us, and then we can—"

Carmella pulled away from Anita, shaking her head. "Anita . . . wait, please," she said, her breath ragged. "What are you doing? I thought . . . I thought maybe you were caught, arrested . . . but this . . . Black Mamba was just here, ten minutes ago. She saw you on the cameras, Anita! She knows you're with the Avengers, and she's going to *kill* you. What were you thinking?"

"I was thinking of *you*," Anita said, her voice breaking. "The Serpent Society is *not* helping us. Not like they promised. Please, I can explain everything, but you have to trust me when I say that we *cannot* stay here."

Carmella looked at Anita, her chest rising and falling, each breath a wheezing rattle. "I trust you. Of course I do, I just . . ." She grasped at Anita's hands, her chin trembling. "I thought I was going to die here. Alone. But the thought of them finding you and killing you, too, that's so much worse. We're not super heroes, Anita. If we try to fight them, they'll kill us. I know it."

Black Widow clenched her jaw. She turned to the other two and said, "You won't have to fight anyone."

Quantum-Freak looked at her, puzzled. "What do you mean? We still have to get to the laboratory and then out. That's where they're keeping everyone."

"Do you think you have two more portals in you?" Black Widow asked.

"I don't know," Quantum-Freak said. "That last one was rough."

Carmella winced. "It's been too long since your last dose. You shouldn't be creating rifts at all. Black Mamba said—"

"Black Mamba is trying to scoop out our brains and replace them with—with some sort of *thing* that does whatever they say. We can't dose again, ever," Quantum-Freak said. She turned to Black Widow, her wide eyes rimmed with tears. "I can do two portals, I think . . . but that's it."

"Good," Widow said. "Get me out of here, past that vault, and into the lab . . . and then you're done. Make one last portal, and take Carmella back to Stark Tower. We'll meet there once we clean this place up."

Quantum-Freak gaped at her, looking as if she didn't understand. "But . . . after all that, I can't—I can't just leave you alone here."

Black Widow offered her a brief smile. "Get me to where they're keeping Bruce Banner, and I *won't* be alone."

CHAPTER THIRTEEN

GREAT COST

Bruce Banner thought that his mind was playing tricks on him when the room split open before him and Black Widow stepped into it.

He had been flitting in and out of consciousness ever since Puff Adder had tranquilized him, strapped him down, and hooked him up to the machine. Every hour on the hour, a needle would descend and penetrate his neck, drawing out blood in big, sucking gulps. He'd gathered that this was how Black Mamba's young recruits were getting their powers, by some sort of concoction created using the blood of super humans. He originally planned on letting them hold him while Quantum-Freak sought out the Avengers so he could extract as much information as possible, truly believing that she would turn on her employers to save Carmella, but he couldn't let them weaponize his blood. If they were able to synthesize it into something that would make another Hulk, that would be a bigger problem than he was prepared to grapple with.

However, as soon as he was locked onto his gurney,

woozy from the tranq but still able to Hulk out if pressed, a young man with an enlarged forehead and shining black eyes that looked like beetle shells stood over him. Bruce felt as if he'd instantly become weightless as the young man's lips rapidly moved, whispering words that were too soft, too fast for Bruce to understand. He found himself falling into a fugue state—completely calm as the needle pierced his neck for the first time. Knowing that he was being mystically numbed by the black-eyed kid, he had attempted to dip into his well of power, to bring forth the Hulk before the monster inside was too far from his grasp, but he couldn't. He was far from angry. He was at peace, perhaps for the first time since he'd met his other half.

That peace came to an abrupt end when Bruce saw Natasha emerge from the portal, her hand reeling back, clutching her baton. With a flick of her wrist, the baton went flying across the room and out of Banner's sight, hitting its target with a loud crack. Suddenly, a wave of anxiety, terror, and pure, animalistic rage awoke within Bruce Banner, surging inside of him like a wave about to break. He felt his muscles burst free of the straps binding him, and, as his skin hardened, the needle piercing his neck shattered, sending a burst of blood smacking to the floor.

Black Widow turned to him as he let out a pained groan that built to a roar, the Hulk beginning to manifest. Uttering a single phrase, she held out her hand, quieting the beast.

"Not yet."

Bruce, anchored by her words, closed his eyes and let the monster slow down with a few calming breaths. As he did, the rest of the room came into focus. Black Widow was swinging herself over a gurney toward a man in a lab coat who was reaching for his gun. Her boots slammed into his chest, knocking him into another scientist attempting to escape. She kicked the gun away and bounded after the remaining scientist, who was about to escape into the hall. As he grasped the doorknob, she leapt off the ground in a graceful spinning kick, knocking him away from the door. He fumbled at his waistband, reaching for a pistol. Black Widow rolled her eyes and knelt down, twisting his hand to the side, disarming him.

Bruce Banner watched, his eyes still glazed, as she strapped the two scientist to gurneys, not saying a word. As she finished up, he glanced around the room as his vision cleared, and saw that the laboratory was filled with people hooked up to the same contraption that he had been strapped to, needles piercing their necks, drawing blood out of them and into the core of the machines with rhythmic swigs.

Black Widow was bending down, picking up her discarded baton. Next to it, slumped on the floor, was the black-eyed young man, a knot already beginning to rise on his bulbous forehead as he lay unconscious.

Widow came over to Banner and hugged him, holding

him close as he stared around in horror at the rest of the room. "You're okay," she said.

Banner stared at the fallen man on the floor, his mind once again catching up to his current situation. "How did you know to go for him?"

"Educated guess," she said. "And if it wasn't the alien-looking guy keeping the Hulk at bay, I would've cracked everyone here in the head until I found out who was doing it."

"These are stolen powers," Bruce said, parting from Black Widow as he glanced around the room. As the psychic haze of the black-eyed mystic's calming effect continued to lift, he began to recognize more of the other prisoners. Luke Cage was strapped to a table, next to others Banner didn't know. And then, he saw one he knew well.

Spider-Man, a fellow Avenger.

"I know," Black Widow said as Bruce walked over to Spider-Man. "It's sick."

"Nat . . ." he said, pulling the binds off of Spidey. He couldn't believe they got him. That was no small feat. Gently, he withdrew the needle from his friend's neck, which left a thick hole that sizzled with whatever numbing agent was being administered to the puncture. "They got my blood. They—"

Black Widow moved around the room, freeing the rest. "We can't agonize over that now. We have to get back outside the building. The Avengers need us."

She pulled the needle out of an elderly woman's neck and paused for a second, looking at the hole left behind in the skin. The woman awoke with a soft, gasping breath, and Black Widow backed up, her eyes still trained on the gaping neck wound.

Spider-Man began to stir, letting out a groan, and so Bruce moved to the next prisoner. As he undid Luke Cage's straps and removed the needle, he looked over as Black Widow continued to stare quizzically at the wound on the woman's neck.

"What is it, Nat?" Bruce asked.

"I've seen this type of wound before," Black Widow said, moving to the next prisoner with a newfound fire in her step. Bruce recognized the man she stood above as Carl "Crusher" Creel, also known as the Absorbing Man, a villain that he had gone up against many times before. It wasn't just the heroes being used and exploited for their powers. It was their enemies as well.

"Keep him strapped down," Banner cautioned.

"I know," Black Widow said. "Heroes go free, baddies are gift wrapped for S.H.I.E.L.D. once we clean this place up." As she withdrew the needle from the villain's neck, she examined the tip of it, nodding. "This is how they did it. I don't know why it killed him and not the people here, but this is it."

"What? Killed who?"

"Paulie Chase," Black Widow said. "The Serpent Society was involved in his murder. He was stabbed in the neck, and his wound looked *just* like these . . . but worse."

"What does that mean?" Bruce said as he removed the needle from Dr. Jonathon Ohnn. Ohnn was one of Spider-Man's foes, and was known for his ability to open black portals in the sky, from which he could attack his enemies from multiple angles. He knew where *this* guy's blood had gone. His ability wasn't perfectly similar to Quantum-Freak's power, but then again, Phononeutria's power seemed somewhat related to Spider-Man's, though not a carbon copy, and the same for the Absorbing Man and Deandre.

"The Maggia is involved in this," Black Widow said. "I don't know to what extent, but we can't wait around here to find out."

Spider-Man sat up on his gurney, rubbing his neck. "Aggghhh . . . ow. Is that Black Widow's voice I hear? Tell me that is Black Widow's voice."

"Rise and shine," Black Widow replied.

"My hero," Spider-Man replied, his voice still heavy from his mystical dream state.

As they freed the rest of the prisoners, Black Widow caught Bruce and Spidey up on the situation. Spider-Man was unsure how long he'd been down there, but remembered being ambushed by a large group of Serpent Society members while stopping a mugging.

"Yeah!" Spider-Man said, rifling through the various cabinets in the laboratory. "So, I'm in the middle of gluing this mugger to a brownstone. Real nasty guy, got more knives on him than teeth. I'm doing my thing, you know, throwing out a few well-placed quips, and all of a sudden a guy dressed like a snake comes out of nowhere! Wait a second . . . YES!" He pulled his web-shooters from a cabinet, snickering as he strapped them on. "They can lock me up and suck my blood, but they shall not take my web-shooters! I mean, I don't want them to do any of that, buuuut that train has kinda passed, am I right?"

Banner gave a puzzled Luke Cage—otherwise known as Power Man, and for good reason—a hand up. Luke asked, "Where am I?"

"You're in a laboratory where someone managed to stick a needle into your unbreakable skin," Banner said. "So, no place good."

"Well, son of a . . ." Luke said, patting at his neck. "It was that freaky lookin' kid with the alien eyes, wasn't it? I felt my skin tingling when he stood over me . . . and not in a good way."

Spider-Man looked at Black Widow, as she did a last check around the room to make sure there were no more imprisoned heroes. "At least you're listening," he said. "So, then a SECOND snake dude comes behind me, and then, before I know it, a snake LADY is there. I'm fighting, shooting webs, insults are flying, and the next thing I know, I'm in a lab trying to tell a super-engaging story to friends who aren't listening."

Banner patted Spider-Man on the back. "Let's go."

"What about these guys?" Spidey asked, motioning to the tranqed super villains. "We can't just . . . you know, leave 'em. Can we?"

"I can," Luke said.

"S.H.I.E.L.D. will be here to clean up," Black Widow said. "With Big Eyes over there knocked out, some of them will be coming to soon. I'd rather get out of here before we have an entirely new set of problems."

"Agreed," Banner said. "Let's move."

Leaving the villains tied to their gurneys, Black Widow led Bruce, Luke Cage, Spider-Man, and a small group of super humans that they didn't know into the dark hallway, which, at first glance, seemed to be deserted. While it was certainly risky walking through the facility with a group they didn't know, they couldn't leave these people behind with a room full of people they knew *for sure* were evil. With Spider-Man, Luke, and Banner back and approaching full strength, they didn't think they'd run into many problems from the folks they were rescuing. It was the Serpent Society and their lackeys they had to look out for.

As they turned a bend, they heard a rustle coming from the other end of the hall, toward the stairs, and turned to see a man in a white lab coat rushing for the flight of stairs.

"Science guy in an evil science lab," Spider-Man said, lashing out his wrist. A burst of webbing shot forth, knocking the scientist's arm against the wall and gluing it there. "Gonna maybe go out on a limb and say he's not down here saving lives."

As the four heroes approached the writhing, screaming man, he pulled and pulled on the webs that plastered his hand to the wall, but it was no use. There were very few that could easily break free of Spider-Man's webbing, and this balding, beady-eyed scientist was not one of them.

"Hi!" Spider-Man said, cocking his head at the whimpering lab coat. "I was just wondering, can you maybe point me toward the guy who strapped me down and stuck a big honkin' needle in my neck? If I had to describe him, I'd say white coat, not so much with the hair situation, maybe a bit of web on his hand? You see a guy like that?"

"Pl-pl-please don't kill me!" the scientist stammered.

Bruce Banner walked up to him, his jaw clenched. "We're not going to kill you. It's your employers who do that sort of thing."

"I could hit you, though," Luke Cage said. "I wouldn't lose a wink of sleep at night. So get to talking before I start taking out my frustration. And let me tell you, I'm feeling mighty frustrated."

"Yeah!" Spidey said, leaning over his shoulder. "Mighty frustrated."

"I've got this, man," Luke Cage said.

"Oh," Spidey said, nodding. "Yeah, of course. Threaten away. Do your thing. I'm cool here."

The scientist, looking from Luke to the others, stammered as he spoke. "I-I had to, I—my wife, they threated to—"

"You didn't have to," Bruce said. "But I understand that the Serpent Society has been offering . . . medical help, of a sort, in exchange for certain services. Was it you who created the serum?"

"Th-there is no one serum," the scientist said, trembling before them. "Every sample is singular. Every batch of b-blood reacts differently to the base. Which, y-yes, I created. Some blood samples we can more easily bind to the base, while others must be altered."

"And that alien-looking guy," Luke said. "He's a product of your experiments down here?"

The scientist nodded. "H-he mutes power," he said. "Anything, from naturally occurring abilities to mystical enchantments, his injections allow him to silence the powers of others."

"And that itself was a stolen power," Black Widow said, shaking her head. "You've endangered countless lives here."

The scientist let out a shaking sob. Luke shook his head.

"The serum . . . is there an antidote to its effect?" Bruce asked.

The scientist looked up at him through wide, bloodshot eyes. His expression said it all.

Banner turned to Black Widow, Luke, and Spider-Man. "Let's go find the rest of the Avengers. I'm feeling the need to work out some aggression myself, and I think it best I remove myself from this man before I do something I regret."

The scientist let out a gasping whimper. Spider-Man, rolling his eyes, held out his wrist, gluing the man's lips shut with a burst of webbing.

"Spidey, Luke . . . you in?" Bruce asked.

Luke looked over his shoulder at the small group of super humans following them, waiting for instructions. "Yeah. I'm in. These folks need someone to keep 'em safe. Best to stick together. Way I see it, we're going to run into some trouble on the way out no matter how this goes down."

"I'm kinda really hoping we do," Spidey said. "I feel like they popped a straw in me and drank me like a Coke. Someone needs to answer for that. I am a man. Not a soda."

Together, the four heroes and the group of nervous super humans moved up the stairs, with Widow and Luke in front, and Bruce and Spidey at the rear. Bruce looked back at the scientist and, while his rage hadn't subsided, he knew that the trembling man was not much different from Quantum-Freak, or most of the other people walking around in the Serpent Society's employ with stolen powers. Under Black Mamba's leadership, the Serpent Society had found a group of people who were being left to suffer by society, and had offered them a solution. Though the cost may have been great, Bruce Banner wasn't entirely sure he could fault them for accepting it.

* * *

As the sun set over the Serpent Society's lair, a sleek, black aircraft that looked like something between a hovercraft and a personal jet launched into the darkening sky from behind the building. Hidden from any technology by a mystical cloak provided by one of the Serpent Society's serum-empowered lackeys, the craft cut through the night sky with little more than a whisper, escaping the notice of the Avengers, who had their hands full with the battle below. From Black Mamba's vantage point out of the craft's side window, the fight against her own personal Hulk was not going the Avengers' way.

"Lovely," she said, tapping her sharpened nails on the glass as the facility quickly fell away into the darkness below.

Black Mamba walked away from the window and settled into her leather seat at the head of a circle of chairs in the main area of the craft. She completed the circle here, which consisted of her current inner circle of Serpent Society members. It was a new hierarchy under her direction, and one that had caused an uproar with long-term members. However, despite the infighting her election and subsequent choices had caused, she felt vindicated by the results. Under the guidance of the previous leaders, all of whom Black Mamba had served loyally and without question at the time, she had seen the Serpent Society squander every opportunity to become a true power in the world of organized crime. Foolish schemes, high aspirations with no hard work, and misplaced vendettas had made them into a laughing stock, but no more.

Even with the betrayal of one of their underlings and the unexpected arrival of the Avengers, the Serpent Society remained incredibly close to completing the first phase of Mamba's plan to make it the most powerful crime syndicate in the embattled underworld of New York City . . . and then, the country. And then . . . the thought of what followed made her lips curl into a cruel smile.

In the circle sat three members of the Serpent Society who had gone to great lengths to earn their place with Black Mamba on this craft. They were once, just like Mamba herself, seen as nothing more than soldiers, grunts following the commands of previous leaders like Viper, who had since abandoned them, and Sidewinder, who had admitted defeat and had since renounced his position of power. With her three confidants, Black Mamba envisioned a world that spoke of the Serpent Society with fear and reverence.

It would take time to gain the latter, but she planned on earning the former that very night.

To her right sat the Asp, who was one of the most physically powerful members of the Society. Her body constantly radiated energy, which she could manipulate into paralyzing blasts called venom bolts. Though Black Mamba had left the concept of equality between herself and the Asp behind when she stepped up to take control of the failing Serpent Society, the Asp was still the closest thing she had to a friend. Like Mamba, the Asp wore a green headpiece, along with a white garment emblazoned with a graphic of two snakes entwined.

Next to the Asp sat Bushmaster, who had lost both arms and legs in an earlier attempt to escape the police. He had been equipped with bionic limbs, including a tail that was appropriately like a snake's in both appearance and proportionate strength. Along with the Asp, he had proven his loyalty to Black Mamba over the years, both in his time fighting alongside of her and now, working directly under her.

Finally, rounding out Black Mamba's inner circle, was Anaconda, one of the founders of the original Serpent Society. Though Anaconda may have believed that Black Mamba kept her close for her expert insight, Mamba in truth couldn't value her opinion less. It was Anaconda's incredible physical power that had gained her the final seat in the inner circle, a position that, though it remained unspoken, the others knew functioned as that of a glorified bodyguard. A hulking mass of muscle, Anaconda looked almost like Thor's female counterpart, but there was something far more bizarre about her powers than the Asgardian Avenger's. Anaconda was able to expand and retract her limbs, allowing her to engorge them into gigantic, snakelike masses of flesh and muscle, manipulating the size and length of her arms and legs.

"All of our hard work, all of our research," Bushmaster said, his tone venomous as he looked past Black Mamba through the window of the craft. "We're abandoning it, aren't we?"

Black Mamba glared at him. "We have the serum. And, more importantly, *I* have a plan."

The others looked at Black Mamba, waiting for her to continue, and she relished the moment of silence. So long had she listened to others, attempting to make good on plans in which, even as a fledgling member, she could see the glaring flaws. She had robbed so many banks, attempted so many minor schemes that did nothing but earn them another beating from Captain America. Now, it was her turn to demonstrate exactly what the Serpent Society could become under good leadership. *Her* leadership.

"The mystical parasite within the serum is engineered to be traceable," Black Mamba said, crossing her legs. "As long as the user is alive, we will be able to *find* them."

"Quantum-Freak turned her back on us," Anaconda said through gritted teeth. "We should kill her, along with her girlfriend. M-80 wasn't strong enough to withstand the serum anyway."

"We are going to find them," Black Mamba said, "but we are *not* going to kill them. Not yet."

"She won't follow through with the original plan, will she?" the Asp asked softly. After all of these years living with the Serpent Society, her Egyptian accent was beginning to fade, but Black Mamba still remembered how she had sounded when they first met. Everything about her had been unique, and still was—though she had been an exotic dancer in her birth country, to Black Mamba, she was nothing short of a princess.

"She won't have a choice," Black Mamba said. She looked from the Asp, to Bushmaster, to Anaconda, studying each of them. "You see, this is where we have failed in the past. The Serpent Society has long been a group of prideful soldiers, and that pride has led to our defeat time and time again. In the past, we would have stood our ground, launching a full—and final—assault on the Avengers, knowing full well that they would take us down. Why? To spit in the face of a hurricane, only to have the wind sent our own saliva back at us?"

Anaconda cocked her head to the side. "When did that happen?"

"It's a metaphor," Bushmaster droned, the contempt plain on his face.

Black Mamba continued. "If the Serpent Society is to rise and claim that which we have always sought—the respect and fear of the world—then we are to *pick* our battles. Beating the Avengers here doesn't matter. Saving our facility doesn't matter. Keeping our prisoners doesn't matter. Not in the least. We already have what we want. We have our rifts . . . and soon we will have our bomb again. Tonight, we will take Quantum-Freak back into our fold and we will march up to S.H.I.E.L.D.'s headquarters."

The other three stared at her, held rapt by her words.

"And we will rip open the sky and swallow it whole, before the world's watching eyes," Black Mamba said, her eyes gleaming. "And then . . . *then* the Serpent Society will rise."

CHAPTER FOURTEEN

A WORLD OF NOTHING

The meaty, green fist slammed into Captain America's face. Again, again. Each time, the bladed bones jutting out from the creature's knuckles barely missed Cap. Dazed, blood streaming down his nose, Cap blocked what may have been the creature's final, devastating punch with his shield, which let off a ringing reverb.

The monster, grunting in confused fury, grabbed the shield. Cap held as tightly as he could as the monster wrapped his fingers around it, but it only took two pulls before he wrenched the shield out of Cap's hands and sent it spinning over the parking lot. It slammed into War Machine's face, taking him out of the sky.

At the last minute, a worn, beaten Captain America was yanked away as the hulking creature's next punch turned the stone below him into rubble.

"Come on, Cap," an equally beaten Hawkeye said, pulling his friend to his full height. "He's the only one left. We got this."

Iron Man, whom Cap had seen thrown across the parking

lot seconds before, sped back toward the beast with Thor and Falcon flanking him, soaring over the unconscious bodies of the gang that had stopped their entry.

"Ready?" Iron Man said.

"Ready," Falcon replied.

"Aye!" Thor bellowed.

The monster lifted its hands, roaring as it prepared to bring both fists down on Cap and Hawkeye, who stood their ground, legs bent, ready to fight the overpowered creature until the end. Cap had been sure that the monster would expend its stolen powers sooner or later, like what was happening to Quantum-Freak, but it was wilder, more vicious than the Hulk that fought alongside of him on the Avengers. He didn't know which it would expend first—its own energy, or the Avengers'.

"NOW!" Iron Man commanded.

The monster brought its balled fists down and Cap and Hawkeye threw themselves to the side, while Iron Man shot a repulsor beam at the monster. Flying just out of the creature's leaping reach, Iron Man circled the sky above, aiming the beam squarely at the monster, forcing the fake Hulk to buckle down as the energy pushed him backward. With every step back the monster took, Iron Man descended lower and lower to the ground, until he was across the parking lot, level with the monster, forcing it backward with his repulsor.

Falcon, ready to fulfill his part of their last-minute plan, brought his wings in against his body and dipped in an arc below the beast. He slammed into the back of the creature's legs, forcing its knees to bend. As soon as it stumbled backward over Falcon and its feet were in the air, Iron Man's repulsor picked him up. The repulsor beam, doubling in strength as Iron Man kicked up his power, sent the monster flying back toward the building. Thor, waiting in the sky, swung Mjolnir above him until it became a blur. As the monster shot past him, propelled forth by Tony's beam, Thor let the hammer fly. It followed the trail of the beam and slammed into the monster's chest, right where the beam was pushing him.

The monster was sent rocketing toward the building, the front of which was obliterated in a shower of bricks, wood, and glass. The fake Hulk, slumped under the pile of rubble, lay still. For a tense moment, the Avengers stood their ground, preparing for the monster to get back up, but when the otherwise silent scene was filled with a thunderous snore coming from the unconscious creature, they exploded in nervous laughter.

Thor, grinning widely, clasped hands with both Iron Man and Falcon as they landed on the ground. Captain America, wiping the blood off of his face, reached down to help a groaning War Machine up.

"That shield," Rhodey said. "It's . . . not soft."

Cap grabbed the shield and put it behind his back, clicking it into place. "No, it's not. You good?"

"Yeah," Rhodey replied, rolling his shoulders. "Maybe a minor case of a broken face, but otherwise . . ."

"*Your* face is broken?" Cap said with a wide grin, pointing at his own. "Want to compare, friend?"

"Uh, guys . . ." Hawkeye said, pulling back a fist full of arrows in his bow. "I'm seeing movement."

Captain America and War Machine looked toward the building. Iron Man, Thor, and Falcon stepped up next to them, lining up in front of Hawkeye. Absurdly, the snore coming from the unconscious monster was turning into a snarling roar as its arms shook, sending the rubble skittering away.

"Looks like the rent-a-Hulk hasn't gotten enough," Iron Man said. He glanced over at Captain America, gesturing toward his face. "Hey, the red looks good on you, Cap. Sort of like a ginger-beard thing going on. Only, you know, made of blood."

"Thanks, Tony. Very helpful," Cap said. He pointed toward the rocks. "Hawkeye, as soon he gets up, make it rain arrows. I don't want to take the chance that he transforms back into his un-Hulked self before we strike. We have to be careful with these kids."

"Yeah," Hawkeye said. "They're all just so fragile."

Cap ignored the comment. "Iron Man and Thor—I don't

want him hitting the building again. We've got people in there, and if we do any damage beyond the door, considering this thing's weight, we could make this place collapse on them."

"Was just gonna say the same thing," Iron Man said. "I think of these things. Don't think I don't think of these things."

"Hit him again, but this time, get above him. Shoot him down at the ground, from different directions, as far away from the building as possible. Then, Rhodey, you light him up. Falcon—Black Widow and Quantum-Freak have been gone for a while. Too long. As soon as the entrance is clear, give me a boost. You and I are going in. We—"

The monster emerged from the rubble of the building's front door with a roar, throwing himself into the air. However, just as Hawkeye unleashed his arrows, the front of the building exploded outward. A blur of green shot toward the Avengers and, for one terrifying moment, it seemed that there was yet another villain for hire juicing on the Hulk serum. However, the second green monster—this one bigger, and with a familiar face—barreled into the first creature, taking it out of the sky. Together, they hit the ground with a tremendous crash, sending a deep crack through the pavement.

Cap held his hands out, stopping the Avengers from following through on his plan as the Hulk, faster and stronger than his copy, wrapped his hands around the fake Hulk's foot.

"He's back," Cap said, grinning.

The Hulk hoisted the writhing monster into the air and began spinning, low and close to the ground, lifting him higher with each 360-degree turn, until the monster was over his head, a gigantic green blur of a halo.

Black Widow, Spider-Man, Luke Cage, and a group of the most thoroughly astonished people any of the Avengers had ever seen walked out of the rubble that was the front door. They stared in awe as the Hulk swung his copycat over his head.

"Sweet Christmas," Luke Cage said, stunned.

"That's my move," Thor said proudly, pointing at Hulk. "He's doing my move! Look how impressive it is."

Then, the Hulk leapt high into the sky, still spinning the creature. When his leap reached its apex, he lurched forward, throwing the creature toward the ground with a roar that seemed to fill the night. As the monster slammed into the ground, cement and dirt kicked up in a tremendous wave. The Avengers turned away from the explosion, shielding their eyes from the shards of stone ripping past them.

The Hulk landed before the crater, already beginning to shrink in size.

They walked through the dust toward the silhouette of Bruce Banner, who had transformed back into his human state. He stood over the gigantic crater, which took up a good quarter of the parking lot, staring down at the muscle-bound man who was splayed out at the bottom of the pit, snoring heavily.

"Huh," he said, breathing heavily as the Avengers stood before him, amazed. Black Widow, her eyes wide, approached him from the building, followed by Spider-Man, Luke Cage, and their group of escaped prisoners, who gaped at the destruction. "I guess I got a little angry there."

* * *

"Coffee?"

Quantum-Freak shook her head as F.R.I.D.A.Y. sent the coffee robot toward her with a tray holding a brand-new pot of coffee, creamer, and sugar. Next to her on the couch in Stark Tower's penthouse, Carmella reached for the pot.

"Do you really think you should be having coffee now?" Quantum-Freak asked.

Carmella, pouring herself a cup with shaky hands, shot Quantum-Freak an expression that she knew to mean *Really?*

Quantum-Freak sighed. "Sorry. I'm just . . . I kinda can't believe we got out of there safely. I keep worrying that . . ."

Carmella settled into the crook of Anita's arm. "That I'm going to lose my cool and blow up the Avengers' living room? I still might. They don't call me M-80 for no reason."

"Stop. I *never* want you to do that again. Last time, you were—"

"I won't," Carmella said. "I don't think I *can* anyway. No juice. I haven't dosed since you did. But don't think you can distract me . . . really, what's worrying you?"

"I'm worried that something's going to go wrong."

Carmella looked up at her. "Me too."

"Do you think I was right?" Anita asked. "To go to the Avengers?"

Carmella breathed in, and Anita could hear her wheeze returning. When they'd begun the injections, it was instantly gone, but now . . .

"I know you did what you thought was best," Carmella said. "I think . . . if you would've asked me at the facility, what I thought we should do, I would *not* have said that going to the Avengers was a good idea. But here we are. Getting served coffee by robots in Tony Stark's penthouse. Kinda crazy."

"Yeah?"

"Yeah," Carmella said. "I think there's still a lot to figure out. And yeah, there's a lot of ways this could go wrong. But we were not in a good place. You did the right thing."

Quantum-Freak nodded. "I hope."

What Quantum-Freak didn't say, though, as she held Carmella close in the comfort of the penthouse, was that this was the nearest she had felt to *okay* in a long time. They still had a host of problems, not the smallest of which was that Black Mamba and the Serpent Society would want their heads on pikes, and that they had been infected with a parasitic agent in the serum that was meant to heal Carmella . . . but at this very moment, with the Avengers out there fighting for them and with Tony Stark's promise that he'd help fresh on her mind, Anita began to allow herself, for the first time since she could remember, to begin thinking about her future with Carmella.

Suddenly, they had tomorrow.

"F.R.I.D.A.Y.," Anita said softly, and the robot rolled its way back toward her. "I actually think I will have a cup of—"

By the time she heard the glass shatter, the thick, powerful hands had already wrapped around her neck. She couldn't see who was attacking her, but in her attempt to free herself, she threw herself to the side and saw that Carmella was being grabbed, too, by an impossibly long, thick, snakelike arm that stretched into the room from outside, through the shattered tempered glass. Struggling against the tightening grip, Quantum-Freak looked through the window, along the length of the arm that dragged her across the penthouse.

The arm extended to what looked at first like a normal, if very flat, jet—but as she was dragged closer, Quantum-Freak could see that it was suspended in midair outside of the penthouse, four thick streams of energy shooting out of ports on its underside. It was a hovercraft.

Anaconda, a wicked gleam in her eyes, stood on top of the craft, her hair whipping wildly in the wind, pulling Anita and Carmella toward the window as she laughed.

"No! They're here!" Carmella screamed.

Anita waved her hands, desperately trying to tap into any residual energy as Anaconda's vice-grip dragged her and Carmella toward the window, but nothing appeared between her fingers but a small line of red energy, no more potent than a static shock. She was spent, unable to open a portal, unable to defend herself or her girlfriend.

"F.R.I.D.A.Y.!" Quantum-Freak screamed. "Help!"

F.R.I.D.A.Y. was already on it. The coffee-bot's chest opened up to reveal a repulsor lens, which shot a flurry of beams at Anaconda's engorged arms—but the villain was too quick. With one final pull, Anaconda pulled Carmella and Quantum-Freak through the window, which exploded in a shower of heavy chunks of glass around them. Carmella screamed as the glass rained down on the busy streets of New York below, but Quantum-Freak's jaw was clenched in silent terror as the harsh wind stung her face. Anaconda held her in midair, the cityscape stretched out below them, and Quantum-Freak knew that all Anaconda had to do was let go, and she would be nothing but a memory.

Quantum-Freak closed her eyes and reached out a shaking hand, hoping it could reach Carmella. She closed her fist around nothing but air.

The hovercraft took off, just as another flurry of repulsor power shot out of the windows. This time, as the wind picked up velocity and she found herself and Carmella trailing behind the craft, suspended helplessly over the city below by Anaconda's hand around their necks, a familiar voice, sharp with fury, boomed from a sound system coming out of the jet.

"Scream until your throats are raw. You don't get to die yet," Black Mamba said, her voice blaring from a speaker within the hovercraft. "You have one more thing to do for me first."

* * *

One terrifying ride through the skies of New York City later, and Anita and Carmella were tossed roughly to the ground as the Serpent Society's hovercraft began to land. When it touched down on the grass below, which blackened from the heat, Anaconda, still laughing, jumped off, her arms retracting to their normal size with a series of wet pops and hisses. She stood over the two young women, who crawled across the grass toward each other.

"Go on," she said, a wicked glint in her eyes. "Get in one last hug."

Behind her, the door on the side of the jet opened, and a retractable staircase extended. Bushmaster and the Asp exited, both armed with dully glowing shotguns emblazoned with the same green serpent on Black Mamba's hairpiece.

Black Mamba herself followed after them, taking slow, purposeful strides down the steps. She carried a briefcase, black except for a snake emblem that matched the design of her hairclip, the metallic and green surface of which reflected the moonlight.

For the first time since landing, Quantum-Freak looked at their surroundings. They had landed just outside a fenced lot, where, in the distance, a sleek, gigantic building reached for the starry sky.

The fence was lined with signs, all boasting the same warning: DO NOT ENTER—GOVERNMENT PERSON-NEL ONLY. Below the words, Quantum-Freak's eyes were drawn to the logo. A familiar eagle.

S.H.I.E.L.D.'s eagle.

"Hold them still," Black Mamba said softly. Anaconda wrapped her arms around Quantum-Freak's writhing form, pulling her away from Carmella, who was seized by the Asp. Quantum-Freak screamed and struggled against Anacon-da's grasp, until the Asp, one arm hooked around Carmella's neck, held the gun to Carmella's head with the other hand. Quantum-Freak shut her mouth instantly, freezing in Ana-conda's grasp.

"Good girl," the Asp said.

Silently, Black Mamba passed the briefcase to Bushmaster

and opened its latches. As she lifted the lid, a cloud of cold gas hissed out. She breathed it in, smiling lightly.

When the gas cleared, Quantum-Freak saw Black Mamba reach into the briefcase. "You betrayed me," she said, withdrawing a syringe, the vibrant orange liquid within lighting her face with a fiery glow. "One of you will die for that."

She approached Carmella with the syringe. The Asp grabbed Carmella's arm, forcing it out for Black Mamba to choose a vein.

"I am going to give you the chance, however, to earn two things," she said. She traced the top of the needle over Carmella's vein, which responded, pulsing over her taut muscles. Black Mamba plunged the needle deep and pressed the neon orange serum into Carmella's blood. "Carmella can earn her *life*. Whatever bit of it remains. And you . . ."

She turned toward Anita as Bushmaster withdrew a second syringe. Black Mamba glared at her as Anaconda ripped back Anita's sleeve, exposing her arm for Bushmaster.

"You, Anita . . . Quantum-*Freak*," she said, spitting the last word. "You can earn yourself a *quick* death."

Anita ripped her arm away from Bushmaster, who approached her with the needle. "You'll kill us anyway. Go to hell."

"Hmm," Black Mamba said. "And here I thought you'd do *anything* for your girlfriend. I suppose I was wrong."

Quantum-Freak looked from Black Mamba to Carmella, from whose skin steam began to rise. Her heart beating fast, her panic rising as Carmella's body was once again exposed to the serum, Anita looked up, past Bushmaster, toward the sky. She took in a long breath, and closed her eyes.

"Anything," Quantum-Freak repeated, and held out her arm.

"Understand," Black Mamba said, "that if I even have the slightest inkling that you're going to attempt to turn on me once again, M-80 dies. Instantly. You know I have the power to do so."

Quantum-Freak nodded. "I understand."

Bushmaster stabbed the needle into her flesh, and the hot, orange liquid flowed into her bloodstream, making her veins burn.

Satisfied, Black Mamba backed up, addressing the Serpent Society. "It is time that we stake our claim," she said. "M-80 . . . you will turn yourself over to S.H.I.E.L.D. Confess. Everything."

"Wh-what should I say?" Carmella asked.

"Tell them," Black Mamba hissed, "the *truth*. Blame me. Tell them my plans, where I am, ask them to help you. Don't hold back. When you are being escorted to tell your story, when you are surrounded by the most people, all at once . . . that is when you will finally be of use to me. That is when you become my bomb."

Anita looked at Black Mamba incredulously. "You can't be serious. You want her to—"

"*Combust,*" Black Mamba cut in. "*That* will be our distraction. In the meantime . . . Quantum-Freak, you will be working on the *real* attack. Open one, final portal. I pushed you to reach across the veil between worlds, between realities, so that you can bring forth things of great power. I had plans for you . . . and I will indeed have plans for your replacement. For now, I ask one final thing of you. Find me a horrible, hellish world. A world of *nothing.*"

Quantum-Freak looked at Black Mamba, her jaw clenched so tight that her face hurt. "Okay," she seethed through gritted teeth.

"When the portal is at its maximum strength and size, move it over the building . . . while they panic after M-80's detonation, you will have the time to bring the portal down over the entire facility. Swallow all of S.H.I.E.L.D., close those fascists in the rift, send them all into oblivion. If you can do this, M-80 lives."

"She'll be *in* the building," Quantum-Freak said.

"Once you begin lowering the portal over the facility, I'll send Anaconda in," Black Mamba said. "She'll pull M-80 out."

"How can I trust your word on that?" Anita asked.

"You'll be in control of the portal, of course," Mamba snapped. "If she doesn't withdraw M-80, you won't complete the mission. Are we *clear*?"

"One last question. What about me?" Quantum-Freak asked.

"Like I said. You die. Quickly," Black Mamba said. "Executed as a symbol of those who betray the Serpent Society. Non-negotiable."

"Anita, *NO!*" Carmella screamed.

Anita stared at Carmella, defeated. "Carm . . . I have to."

Black Mamba tossed her head back and let out a barking laugh. The Asp grinned widely, sharing a triumphant glance with her leader. At that very moment, when Anita was sure that no one else was looking, she stared directly into Carmella's eyes.

And winked.

"Go," Black Mamba said, motioning for Carmella to walk. "Your explosion will be Quantum-Freak's signal to move the portal over the building. With this fresh batch, you will be able to regenerate as soon as you combust. Do you understand?"

Carmella stammered, looking from Black Mamba to Anita. "I—I, er . . . yes. Yes."

The Asp shoved her, and Carmella stumbled forward. She shared one, final desperate look with Anita, who stared back, a newfound calm in her eyes.

Carmella began to climb the fence, and Black Mamba took Anita by the hair, pulling her away from Anaconda. She threw Quantum-Freak to the floor, standing over her.

"Do it," she snapped. "Begin preparing the portal. And make sure *nothing* comes out on this side. Find the emptiest, most desolate world in existence . . . and then, when you hear your girlfriend go *boom*, send our enemy there. And remember . . . one false move, and the deal is off."

Anita twirled her fingers, and felt her power come alive once again with a thick crackle of red energy, which reflected in her gaze. She looked Black Mamba in the eyes and nodded.

"Thank you," she said through gritted teeth.

Quantum-Freak spread her arms, and the sky surged with red energy, which began to tear open an impossibly black hole in the sky. Black Mamba looked up at the portal with admiration, bathing in the crimson light.

"Incredible," she said as wind burst forth from the portal, which expanded above them, growing from the size of a window, to the size of a car, to the size of a truck . . .

Black Mamba narrowed her eyes as she heard an engine rev from within the portal.

"Oh, just wait," Quantum-Freak said, ripping the sky open with her power. "It gets better."

CHAPTER FIFTEEN

SERPENT

Thor and the rest of the Avengers were loading back into the Humvee outside the abandoned mental facility, the front of which had been reduced to rubble. It was dark, the only light coming from the moon and the Humvee's headlights, which shone bright beams of golden light on the wreckage of the parking lot. Luke Cage, Spider-Man, the Falcon, and Redwing were staying behind, waiting for S.H.I.E.L.D. to come pick up the defeated villains that littered the parking lot. As the two groups of heroes were parting, Captain America pulled a grumbling Copperhead out of the car and passed him over to Luke Cage.

"Thanks for handling this, friend," Cap said.

Luke Cage looked down at Copperhead from arm's length, and shook his head. "Can't believe I got duped by a group of people dressing like snakes."

Once their good-byes were said, the Avengers drove off toward Stark Tower, where they planned to meet up with Quantum-Freak and Carmella. With F.R.I.D.A.Y. in control of the car, the mood in the back was light despite the fact that a good number of them had taken quite a beating. Thor took pleasure in that. It seemed, he thought, that they were well on their way to putting this conflict behind them.

Perhaps the time drew close that Thor could finally dine. His stomach's rumble rose against the roar of the Humvee's engine.

"So, on the way out of the facility," Captain America said, looking toward Black Widow and Bruce Banner, "you didn't run into any more members of the Serpent Society?"

"No one. We opened every door we passed," Widow said. "No sign of Black Mamba."

"The assault in the parking lot was probably meant to do more than keep us out of the facility," War Machine said. "I'm thinking they escaped."

"Agreed," Banner said. "Cap, where do you think they would've gone?"

"Alert!" F.R.I.D.A.Y.'s voice chimed in. "There has been an attack at Stark Tower."

Tony shot forward in his seat, his eyes gleaming. "Anita and Carmella—are they okay?"

"Some sort of malware was sent into the penthouse and is working its way through the system," F.R.I.D.A.Y. said. "This attack happened twenty-five minutes ago. All footage is being reviewed, but there are gaps, and–"

"So they one-upped us on the science game, I got it," Tony said. "*What about* Anita and Carmella?"

"They are no longer on site. There is damage to the penthouse, and evidence to suggest that they have been abducted by an enemy craft. Their technological attack on our network was vicious, and messy. By the time you arrive, I will have reassembled security footage and—"

"I'm getting out of here, now," Tony said, cutting her off. "You take the Humvee back. I'm taking to the skies. I'm finding those two, right now."

"Wait," Banner said. "Let's just slow down and think for a moment. They're not *at* the tower, and the Serpent Society is not going to return to their headquarters. Where could they be going?"

As if in answer to Banner's question, the sky ripped open in front of their vehicle.

Thor saw it before anyone else, confused. He shouted, "Ahead!"

F.R.I.D.A.Y. jerked the wheel to the side, but the portal was curving around them in a circle, leaving nowhere to go but inside.

"Grab on to something, now!" Cap yelled, as the front of the Humvee careened into the glowing, expanding rift in the sky.

The Avengers clamped on to what they could, bracing themselves as the Humvee was enveloped in a flash of red, and then darkness. For an extended moment there was nothing but pure black as the vehicle fell through nothingness.

Then, a circle of light at the end came into their line of vision and quickly expanded, flying toward the descending vehicle with great speed.

Thor leaned past the others as what appeared to be cement rushed toward the front of the car. With only a split second to act, Thor charged forward and shot through the windshield, racing to outrun gravity as the Humvee careened toward him.

He landed on solid ground with just enough time to fly back a yard in the air to catch the descending Humvee, an instant before it would've crashed directly into the ground. Thor looked through the shattered windshield to see the other Avengers gaping at him from within the vehicle.

"It was nothing, really," he said, with a grin and a shrug, lifting the Humvee as he did so.

"Thor!" Black Widow called out, reaching for her baton. "Behind you!"

Thor turned around, the Humvee's bumper still in his right hand, just in time to grab the barrel of the Asp's gun with his left. In one fluid arc of motion, he set the Humvee down as gently as possible—which, the Avengers inside later argued wasn't that gently at all—and, still clutching the gun, pulled the Asp forward. She held tightly on to the weapon, which shot a cluster of deadly energy into the sky. With another tug, the Asp came jerking toward him, and he used her momentum to throw her over his shoulder, disarming her.

As the Avengers piled out of the car and Thor stood over the Asp, who scrambled backward as she looked up at the team of heroes, the Avengers took in their surroundings. They were right outside of S.H.I.E.L.D., under one of Quantum-Freak's portals, which was puckering closed above them. Quantum-Freak herself was dashing toward them from a few yards away, as Black Mamba, flanked by Bushmaster and Anaconda, ran after her, S.H.I.E.L.D.'s floodlights sweeping over them.

"I gave you a chance to save Carmella, and you betray me once again?" Black Mamba screamed. "You just earned her a death sentence!"

Iron Man, Thor, and War Machine leapt into the air, flying toward Quantum-Freak, but before they could get to her, Anaconda's arms shot out, tripling their length, and caught Anita's foot. She fell to the ground, hard, and Black Mamba snatched Bushmaster's gun, pointing it down at Quantum-Freak.

"Don't come an inch closer," Black Mamba hissed. "Or I fry her. Right here."

The Avengers came to a sudden stop. Black Mamba held the barrel of the gun at Anita's head, at point-blank range. As fast as they were, all it would take would be the slightest twitch of Black Mamba's index finger. Not even Thor or Iron Man could get to the girl in time.

"Think about what you're doing here," Captain America

said, attempting to keep his tone measured as he faced his old enemies. "All of this, for what? To put on a show? Make a point?"

"To rise," Black Mamba said. "How many times have you interfered in our plans? Spit in our faces? The days of a Serpent Society that folds to Captain America, to S.H.I.E.L.D., to the Avengers . . . those days are long gone. The tides of the resistance are changing, you relic. This is just the beginning."

"Uhhhh, might want to look around," Iron Man said. "You can't win this. Period. Do the math. The moment you pull that trigger, you're done."

"Make a move, then," Black Mamba said. "I will kill this girl and sleep like a baby tonight."

"Please."

The voice came from behind the Serpent Society. Black Mamba didn't dare turn away from the Avengers, but Bushmaster and Anaconda spun around, clearing the Avengers' view to Carmella, her skin glowing red, steam rising off of her body in the cool night, striding toward the parking lot.

"Please don't hurt her," Carmella said. "If you do . . ."

"Carmella," Captain America said. "Don't do it. If you detonate now, you'll—"

"It's her call," Carmella interrupted, punctuating her words with a ragged cough. She turned back to Black Mamba. "We gave you loyalty in exchange for your help. You filled our veins with poison. You threatened to kill us. All

Anita was doing, all she ever did, was look out for me. Try to save me."

"Carmella, go!" Quantum-Freak shouted. "While you still can, please . . ."

"So you're saying . . ." Black Mamba said, pressing the energy gun against Anita's temple, "that I should just let you *both* go."

"I'm saying that you shouldn't expect blind loyalty when you've given us nothing in return," Carmella said, her eyes flashing with red light. "Yes. I'm saying that you should let us go."

The Avengers stood tense, ready to move the moment Black Mamba acted. The Asp stirred in the distance, groaning. Bushmaster and Anaconda faced Carmella, also prepared to attack the moment things went south.

Black Mamba looked from Carmella's pleading gaze to Quantum-Freak, whose jaw was clenched, her wide eyes staring at the night sky above. Black Mamba's eyes bored into Quantum-Freak's, her expression completely unreadable.

The word came out of Black Mamba's mouth softly. A whisper.

"No."

She pulled the trigger, and a ball of crackling energy blasted into Quantum-Freak's skull. As she fell face first, convulsing on the ground as light poured out of her eyes, the Avengers and the Serpent Society acted immediately, knowing all bets were off.

* * *

Iron Man flew right to Carmella, picking her up off the ground and into the air, away from the rest of his friends, who clashed with the Serpent Society below.

"NO!" Carmella screamed, steam rolling off of her, sweat pouring down her face as her body temperature soared. The number displayed on Tony's HUD was unbelievable, and increasing. "PUT ME DOWN! LET ME FACE HER!"

"Not like this," Tony said. "Can't let you do it."

"She ... she ..." Carmella's words died on her lips as Tony brought her higher into the air, away from the clash below.

"I know," Tony said, his eyes shining. "I promise. I *promise* I will do everything I can. But if you go down there and blow it all to hell ... then we've already lost."

Tony looked at her, to make sure that she wasn't preparing to explode, and saw that she was staring wide eyed back toward where Quantum-Freak lay. He followed her gaze to see an enormous bolt of red lightning blast out of Quantum-Freak's body below and shoot into the sky, lighting it up with fiery energy. They watched together as the sky split open—a small rip at first, and then, for a moment, Tony thought she would rip their very plane of existence asunder.

"What's that?" Iron Man said. "What's she doing?"

"I don't think she's doing it on purpose," Carmella said, tears flowing down her cheeks, turning to steam before they reached her chin.

A portal that had to be a city block wide opened above the Avengers and the enormous S.H.I.E.L.D facility. The sounds of fists flying and laser guns going off below, as well as the rising cacophony of the gathering forces of S.H.I.E.L.D.'s aircrafts, which lifted out of the facility and began to head toward the scene of the battle, was drowned out by an ear-splitting, discordant roar that boomed from within the portal.

"Well," Iron Man said, swooping back down the ground, Carmella in his arms. "A sound like that is never good."

"She . . . she mentioned . . ." Carmella stammered, trailing off.

He let go of Carmella as they touched down a safe distance away from the fight. He pointed at her. "Mentioned what? Do you know what's coming out of that?"

Carmella, her eyes wide with tears, nodded. "She's had nightmares ever since she took the injection. There are worlds out there with things that want to . . . to come here. Wicked things. She heard one of the worlds in her dreams, reaching out to her. I think this is it."

Iron Man sighed, looking up at the growing portal as a series of helicopters and fighter jets launched from S.H.I.E.L.D.'s facility. "Yep," he said. "Of course it is."

"Does this mean she's alive?" Carmella asked, her voice hoarse.

Iron Man stared at Carmella for a beat, searching for the words. He'd lied to Quantum-Freak's face earlier, and the memory tore at him. He wouldn't do the same to Carmella. It would be safer to tell her *yes*, to keep her away from the fight, but staring at her here, he just couldn't bring himself to make a promise he knew he couldn't keep.

"Stay back," he said. "If Quantum-Freak . . . Anita, if Anita is . . . whatever happens, Black Mamba will pay. I swear it."

Carmella stared at him as a gargantuan shadow fell over them. "You lied to Anita before. I know you did."

Iron Man stood still as a statue, facing her. "Yeah. I did. But this time, I'm telling the truth."

"As soon as you're gone, you know I'm going to her side," Carmella said.

"I know," Tony said. "But I had to at least say it."

He blasted off the ground and raced back to the Avengers and the Serpent Society, who were watching in horror as the source of the roar began to emerge from the surging portal. The fight between the two clashing sides was seemingly put on halt, as both heroes and villains stood side by side as the moonlight was blotted out by the creature that began to emerge from the portal.

* * *

"Get ready!" Captain America said, grasping his shield. An enormous serpent curled out of the portal, blotting out the moonlight above them and the S.H.I.E.L.D. facility below, which was now flooded with lights as the organization launched into defensive action.

The serpent's head was as big as the Humvee, with pale, shining eyes, and row upon row of sharp, needle-like teeth thicker than Thor's biceps. Its scales were black, dripping wet with heavy glops of tar-like slime. Eight horrific wings, bony and veined, protruded from its spiked spine, and kicked up great torrents of air as it flew out of the portal, its seemingly endless body snaking through the sky above the Avengers. For a moment, as its finned tail pulled free of the portal, it seemed as if the terrible creature would fly off into the night, but instead, it doubled back around, its speed increasing tenfold as it dove toward the Avengers, its enormous mouth opening up as if to swallow them whole.

As it shot toward them, a passing S.H.I.E.L.D. helicopter dipped low, peppering the monster with gunfire. Without changing direction, the serpent whipped its tail around, cutting through the chopper, which exploded in a rush of flames upon impact.

Cap and the other Avengers ran as the creature's jaw smashed into the ground, slicing through the earth like a shark through water. Black Mamba laughed triumphantly for a moment, but the sound turned into a gurgle of confused fear as the serpent's open mouth raced toward her.

Captain America tackled her out of the way as the serpent snapped its jaw shut where she had been standing, taking a chunk out of the ground with its deadly fangs. Black Mamba and Captain America crawled away from its opening mouth as the monster took flight once again.

It rushed past a series of S.H.I.E.L.D. helicopters, which lit up the night with heavy fire. The demonic serpent, seemingly unimpeded by their attacks, continued to move toward them. Iron Man, Thor, and War Machine moved toward it, attempting to draw it away from the S.H.I.E.L.D. choppers, which seemed to be nothing more than target practice for the monster's whipping tail and snapping jaw.

Back on the ground, Captain America pushed himself off of Black Mamba. "I don't think that thing shares your enthusiasm for the Serpent Society," Captain America said.

Black Mamba lifted her gun toward Cap, blasting a cluster of energy at him. He caught the brunt of it on his shield, which vibrated as it absorbed the shock. She followed through with another blast, this time of her own Darkforce energy. The crackling orb of purple and black power shot toward Captain America's legs. He leapt over it but another orb was already coming at his face, which he blocked with the shield, while moving toward her.

As he lowered the shield, he saw Black Mamba spin away from him. She raced across the ground toward the Serpent Society's craft, throwing another orb of Darkforce energy over her shoulder. Cap ducked the orb and dashed after her, shouting to Iron Man, who was drawing the demonic serpent's attention with a series of repulsor blasts. Much to Captain America's dismay, another cluster of helicopters had joined the fray.

"I've got Black Mamba!" Cap called. "Keep the fight in the sky! Contact Maria Hill and tell her to get her people out of here! This thing is going to destroy them!"

"On it!" Iron Man shouted back, though Captain America knew they were both aware that S.H.I.E.L.D. Director Maria Hill would do no such thing. If there was a threat in the sky over the United States of America, much less over her place of operations, she would stop at nothing until she brought it down.

As Cap pursued Black Mamba, he looked up to see War Machine and Thor flanking Iron Man, the trio sending a flurry of missiles, repulsor power, and bolts of lightning at the otherworldly serpent in midair. From behind the monster, a squadron of S.H.I.E.L.D. jets cut through the sky, sending automatic gunfire at the writing monster.

Cap, running toward the fleeing Black Mamba, leapt as the ground behind him exploded. The jets were peppering the ground with gunfire in their attempt to take down the serpent, and Captain America silently prayed that none of the stray bullets hit any of his people.

* * *

In the air, Iron Man aimed a concentrated, blindingly bright repulsor beam at the serpent's face. Thor threw his legs over the creature and began riding it, delivering cracking blows to its spine with Mjolnir. The monster writhed in the sky, as Thor held on to it, hitting the creature over and over with his mighty hammer as War Machine sent guided missiles after it. The explosions sent showers of thick sludge from the creature's wounds down onto the ground, but didn't seem to slow it down. Hawkeye, from the ground, was shooting everything he had at the serpent, from exploding arrows to acid-tipped arrows to arrows with functioning drills on the tips of them.

Iron Man shouted into his HUD as the serpent bit the wing off of a jet. "Director Hill!" he called. "Director Hill, do you hear me?"

Maria Hill's face popped up in the corner of his field of vision in his HUD. He could see that she was holding her phone up as she ran in the facility, and noticed a Helicarrier behind her. Agents of S.H.I.E.L.D. were piling into it, all of them heavily armed and prepared for war.

"Stark, what have you brought to my front door?" Hill snapped.

"Hold on the Helicarrier!" Iron Man shouted. "This thing will bring your people out of the sky with a shimmy of its tail. Let the Avengers handle this one."

"You contacted me while my facility is under attack to tell me to *stand down*," Hill said, fury blossoming on her face. "You're unbelievable, Stark. I'll be out there momentarily and, when I do, *you* will follow *my* orders. Over."

The communication ended, leaving Iron Man's HUD showing nothing but the serpent before him and a flurry of statistics he wasn't even reading. He silently vowed to bring the serpent down before Maria Hill could get that Helicarrier out there.

Rejoining Thor, War Machine, and the growing cluster of S.H.I.E.L.D helicopters, Iron Man rocketed toward the serpent just as it locked its jaws around War Machine's foot. Making a beeline for its mouth, Iron Man held out his gauntlets, aiming directly for the creature's exposed gums as it curled its lip up, attempting to pull War Machine into its mouth with its black, forked tongue.

The repulsor beam shot out of Iron Man's gauntlet and hit its target. The creature opened its mouth in a roar of pain, giving War Machine the chance to blast away from it. However, instead of falling, it looked toward Iron Man with vengeance in its eyes.

"Oh, boy," Tony said as the serpent roared and shot toward him with renewed fury.

* * *

Across the field, Black Widow and Bruce Banner stepped up to Anaconda, Bushmaster, and the Asp, whose eyes were darting from the enormous serpent down to their craft, where Captain America was pursuing Black Mamba.

"Trying to duck out?" Black Widow said, flicking her wrists. Electricity flowed across her bracelets and down to her batons, which she twirled as she lunged at Bushmaster and the Asp, while Banner circled around Anaconda.

"That thing's gonna kill us all," Bushmaster said, swinging his tail at Black Widow.

"And whose fault is that?" she replied, jumping over the tail and launching into a spinning kick, catching Bushmaster in the jaw. She landed and followed through with another kick, which he dodged.

Bushmaster caught her with an uppercut to the chin that lifted her off the ground. She used the momentum, landing on her feet gracefully. Ducking low, she shot out her leg, sweeping the Asp's feet out from under her.

Preparing for another brutal punch, Bushmaster charged toward her. Black Widow feinted to the side just as he threw his fist forward, and then came back at him, flipping onto her hands and launching both feet into his chest. He went flying from the force of the kick, but Widow already had her eye on the Asp. The Avenger landed on her feet, grasping her batons tightly.

The Asp lunged at her, and Widow kicked her in the stomach, setting her up for the next strike. Black Widow came cracking down with both batons on either side of the Asp's collarbone. The Asp let out a gasp of pain, but she didn't go down as quickly as she had against Thor. She head-butted Black Widow, knocking her into the path of Bushmaster's whipping tail. It caught her in the stomach, lifted her into the air, and tossed her, sending her skidding across the ground.

Black Widow wasn't done, though. Shaking off the blow, she raced back over to them and launched into a flurry of kicks, punches, and strikes with her baton, administering shocks to them with every blow landed.

* * *

As Black Widow took on those two, Banner was having the life squeezed out of him by Anaconda, who had wrapped her arms around his torso.

"You're not so tough," she said with a barking laugh, squeezing harder.

"Maybe I'm not," Banner replied, his eyes closed. "But *he*

is." When his eyelids shot open to reveal a pair of bloodshot eyes, his irises glowed a poison green, and his pupils were dilating. Anaconda barely had time to unwrap her arms as Banner's muscles grew, his bones expanding and his skin turning green as he transformed into the Hulk.

Anaconda shot a fist at the Hulk's face, but he ducked as her arm extended to an impossible length as it flew past him like a torpedo. She jerked her shoulder, and the arm shot back into place, knocking Hulk in the face as it returned to its normal size.

He growled, unharmed . . . but furious.

Lashing out a fist, he snatched Anaconda's arm just as she was going for another punch. He pulled her in close, and met her with a punch that knocked her out cold with a single blow. Still holding her limp body, Hulk looked to the sky.

Iron Man, Thor, and War Machine zipped around the serpent, with Hawkeye somehow now on its back. S.H.I.E.L.D. helicopters continued to aim gunfire at the monster that seemed to be even more vicious than it had moments earlier, and was not even slightly hindered by the rain of attacks from both the Avengers and S.H.I.E.L.D. The creature was harmed, but was also angrier, raging across the sky. The Hulk prepared to leap at it, but stopped himself when he spotted Carmella off to the side, cradling Quantum-Freak's body.

He cocked his head to the side, and walked over to them

as Black Widow continued to beat on the Asp and Bushmaster in the background, handling the two villains on her own.

* * *

Captain America hopped up onto the wing of the Serpent Society craft and slid down in front of the door, just as Black Mamba was barreling toward it.

"You're not done here yet," Cap said, slamming his shield into her face. She stumbled backward, but still held on to the gun. She pointed it at Cap, ready to let off another orb of power, but Cap grabbed the barrel and delivered a sharp kick to her elbow, wrenching the weapon from her grasp. He cracked the gun over the wing of the craft, breaking the weapon with a shower of sparking energy, and swung the stock of it at Black Mamba, who blocked his attack with her forearm.

"I will not fold to you," she snapped, holding her hands together to build an orb of Darkforce energy. A familiar face—Bucky Barnes's face—began to form within the energy as Black Mamba expanded her power. "Not ever again."

Cap's eyes widened, and he reached out, grabbing Black Mamba by the arm. She thought she was triumphant, but only for a moment. He pulled her away from the jet, using all of his strength to throw her out of harm's way as the serpent, its great mouth gnashing, flew directly at the hovercraft. It snapped its mouth shut on it, biting the nose off as Iron Man landed a potent repulsor blast in its eye.

"Sorry, Cap!" Iron Man said. "Hard to keep this thing above ground!"

As the serpent arched back up, Captain America stood over Black Mamba, who looked up at him, so angry that he could hear her breath coming out in ragged, shaking hisses. She held on to the Darkforce energy, the telekinetic projection of Bucky's face wavering as she lost her will. Captain America slammed the orb away with his shield, staring down at her with distaste.

"Come on," Cap said.

"I . . . I will never stop," Black Mamba said. "I have true power here . . . you'll see."

"You let people believe you were helping them," Cap said, looking down at her through narrowed eyes. "They gave you their trust."

"And I offered them the world," Black Mamba snapped back.

Cap glared at her. "And look what it got them."

* * *

Black Widow delivered the final few blows to the Asp and Bushmaster as Bruce Banner—shrinking to his normal state with every step—approached Carmella. Quietly, he stood by her side. She held Quantum-Freak, who, despite a vicious burn mark on her neck and head, was breathing. Slow, shallow breaths . . . but alive was alive.

Bruce cleared his throat, and Carmella, clutching the trembling Quantum-Freak, turned to him with shining eyes.

"Your powers," Bruce began. "They never taught you to use them, did they?"

"I don't have any powers," Carmella said. "What they stuck me with . . . I see now, it's nothing but another drug that doesn't work. A lie. This isn't me. I'm not M-80. Anita isn't Quantum-Freak. This is what happens when we think we can just beat the system. We can't. It's not there to be beaten."

"Still, no matter where your abilities came from, you knocked the Hulk out," he said. "And that? That is not easy. It might take something like that to stop that serpent."

Together, they looked up at the monster in the sky. The Avengers fought valiantly and had done visible damage to the monster's face, but it was still attacking with just as much fury as before.

"What do you mean?" Carmella asked. "If I combust again, it'll—"

"Then don't combust," he said. "You have an immense amount of energy built up inside you. And trust me, I know, that kind of thing . . . it just wants to burst out. Uncontrolled, unbridled, just pure and utter rage. It feels like just giving in is the only way to do it."

"What are you saying?"

"Don't give in to the rage," he said. "Reach into it. Dip your fingers in it. Draw from it, and then . . . then, give that monster some hell."

"*I can't*," Carmella said. "I blow up. That's what I do. I'm nothing more than a bomb to them."

"Listen to him . . ." Quantum-Freak wheezed, her eyes cracking open. "He's smart."

Carmella, her jaw trembling, looked from her girlfriend to Bruce. "How?"

"You're looking outward, allowing that power to consume everything about you as it lashes out. Instead, focus inward. Ground yourself. I mean, if Quantum-Freak—if Anita could, you know she'd be doing everything in her power to send that monstrosity back to the dimension it came from."

"I don't know if I can," Carmella said.

"Trust me. This is coming from someone who you exploded on less than twenty-four hours ago. Just because you made a bad choice it doesn't make you a bad person." Bruce held her gaze. "I don't know if you can do it, either. But you can try."

He knelt next to Carmella, helping her gently set Anita down. She had passed out once again, and Bruce silently hoped that she would wake up when all of this was over. Carmella, her eyes red with tears, bent down and pressed a soft kiss onto Anita's forehead before turning around and looking up at the serpent in the sky.

"I'll try," Carmella said softly, reaching out her hands. They glowed red-hot, ready to unleash her flames within.

Next to her, Bruce's skin began to turn green. He nodded to her. "Let's do it together. Remember. Don't let it consume you. Instead, ride it. Just follow my lead."

* * *

Captain America delivered a final knock-out blow to Black Mamba just in time to watch Banner transform into the Hulk. He was next to Carmella, whose hands erupted in two balls of flame . . . both pointed at the writhing serpent in the sky. The monster was now moving toward the S.H.I.E.L.D. headquarters. Beyond the gate, lights were flooding on, and agents on foot and in military vehicles began driving across the lawn.

"We're ending this!" Cap screamed at the top of his lungs, watching with pride as the team, having defeated the Serpent Society, converged on the monster from above and below. "NOW!"

As the serpent opened its mouth, descending on the S.H.I.E.L.D. headquarters below, Iron Man held out both hands, flying backward as he delivered twin beams into the creature's eyes. Thor pointed Mjolnir forward from above, unleashing a steady stream of lightning on the serpent's wings, cutting holes in the veiny membranes with each blinding strike. Black Widow picked up the Asp's discarded energy gun and aimed it expertly at the serpent's eyes, every blast hitting its target even from the great distance. Hawkeye, anchored by an arrow and a cord, swung off the beast's back as War Machine peppered its hide with grenades that popped in flashes of flame on its back. The S.H.I.E.L.D. helicopters continued their assault and, in the distance, Cap saw—to his dismay—a Helicarrier rising up from the facility.

"Go!" Captain America screamed. "Go, go! Don't let it get the Helicarrier!"

The Hulk threw himself into the air with a wild, leaping bound and grabbed on to the serpent's snout. He shoved his beefy hands into the monster's mouth, gripping its lip. With all of his strength, the Hulk forced the serpent's jaw open, exposing the white, fleshy tissue of its tongue and throat, both lined with black slime that covered the Hulk's hands as the other Avengers attempted to line up their shots.

The Hulk jerked the creature to the side, pulling its mouth away from the S.H.I.E.L.D. agents below, and back toward the Avengers as Captain America let his shield fly with a great swing, sending it into the creature's open mouth.

As the choking serpent dipped toward the ground, causing the S.H.I.E.L.D. agents to scatter, Iron Man and Thor continued their attacks, and looked up in surprise when a stream of inconceivably hot flames in the form of a beam shot across the field, through the fence, and into the serpent's mouth. Combined with the power of Iron Man's repulsors and Thor's lightning, Carmella's concentrated stream of flames shot into the serpent's gaping mouth. Its entire body lit up from inside as the Helicarrier moved toward it in the distance. Its scales burst off of its body, flames shooting out from its flesh from inside as it let out a final, pained cry.

"Take cover!" Iron Man said, flying toward the ground. "It's gonna—"

With a ground-shaking explosion, the flames burst out from the monster. Hot chunks of seared serpent rained onto the field, covering the baffled S.H.I.E.L.D. agents, the Avengers, and the defeated Serpent Society.

Carmella dropped her hands and the flames dissipated. Captain America watched her from a distance, as the charred pieces of the monster's remains sent plumes of smoke up into the air around her. He thought to himself that if he hadn't seen the demonic serpent explode in mid-air, the smiling woman surrounded by rising curls of smoke would be a beautiful sight.

Cap, smiling proudly, walked up to Carmella, holding out a hand. She shook it.

"I have no idea what that was," Cap said, picking up his shield, which was covered in thick, smoking black liquid. "But kudos to you for doing it."

Carmella began to smile, but it faded when she looked down and saw that Quantum-Freak was gone. Her eyes frantically scanned the area and settled on two figures by the ruined Serpent Society craft.

"Anita!" she gasped.

Together, she and Captain America ran over to Quantum-Freak, who now stood over Black Mamba, holding her hand out. Red energy crackled from finger to finger, and blasted out of the wound in her neck. Black Mamba had regained consciousness, and looked up at Quantum-Freak with hate in her eyes.

"You know . . . every night since you first gave me the serum, I've had nightmares about that dimension," Quantum-Freak said, pointing to the closing rift in the sky. "There's more than one of that monster, you know. They want out. They can smell us from across the divide. Something tells me they'd love to eat us alive. Maybe I owe them a snack."

"You wouldn't," Black Mamba said, looking up at her from the ground.

"I would," Quantum-Freak said, her energy building.

"Anita, listen . . ." Captain America began. Behind him, S.H.I.E.L.D.'s aircrafts were landing. "You can't do this. I know what she did to you, but look at you . . . you *healed*. Everything is going to be okay. This would—"

"I want to see her suffer," Quantum-Freak continued,

cutting Captain American off as the rest of the Avengers gathered behind him.

Hawkeye slowly, silently pulled an arrow back in his bow. As he lifted it, pointing it at Anita's elbow, Bruce Banner grabbed his arm, giving him a slight shake of the head.

Quantum-Freak glared down at Black Mamba. "Did you hear me? I'd love to see *you* suffer," she said. "But even more than that, I want you to live knowing that you lost."

She closed her fist, extinguishing the red power, and turned to Carmella, throwing her arms around her. The two of them embraced as S.H.I.E.L.D. agents flooded toward them. Director Maria Hill would surely be there soon, and she would have questions that the Avengers were far too tired and hungry to answer, not least of which would be regarding Anita's and Carmella's roles in the night's events. The Avengers knew that there were still loose ends to tie up, but that would all come in time.

For now, their long day was finally over and, for a time, they could rest.

BETTER

Benny the Banger, a beady-eyed man with absolutely no chin but more than enough nose to make up for its absence, was reclined on his sofa in a ratty undershirt and the same tighty-whities he'd worn every other day this week when the front door to his small, Long Island home burst open with a wood-splitting crack.

Fumbling for his bat, he froze in his place when Captain America, decked out in his red, white, and blue uniform, strode into his living room with purpose. His fingers wrapped around the handle of the bat, Benny threw himself off of the couch and darted away from Cap, toward the kitchen. As he grasped at the back doorknob, the door opened in on him with sudden force, cracking him in the head.

Still holding on to the bat, Benny fell back, landing on his rear end as Black Widow, in her sleek uniform, emerged from the door, a baton in each hand. Sunlight streamed in behind her.

"Hello, gorgeous," Benny said, his voice oily.

Black Widow's deadly expression didn't change.

"Do the rest of your men know that you murdered Paulie Chase?" Captain America asked, bearing down on the fallen mobster.

Benny balked at that. "I don't know what you're talkin' about, guy," he snapped. "But you've got me all wrong."

Benny swung the bat upward at Cap, who easily scooted back to avoid the blow. Jumping to his feet, Benny lifted the bat high and opened his mouth in an absurd battle cry, bringing his weapon down over Black Widow. She crossed her batons in the air, catching the bat. Twisting her batons to the side, she pulled it from Benny's arms and sent him sprawling forward toward her. She caught him with a knee in the chest and grabbed the back of his head, pulling back his oily hair.

"The police are outside," Black Widow said. "You're finished. I just wanted to give you the chance to talk."

"It would be smart to listen to her," Cap said. "You see, where you're going, there will be many, many prisoners who remain loyal to Count Nefaria, and to the memory of Paulie Chase. If you were to give the Avengers information regarding your deal with the Serpent Society, we might protect you."

Benny the Banger looked at them with those beady eyes, which shot around the room as if he was trying to calculate his escape. Seemingly deciding that he was stuck, he held up both hands, nodding.

"They came to me, yeah," Benny said. "The snake freaks.

They wanted me to bring in Paulie, 'cause of his powers. You heard the rumors about him. I guess they did, too."

"Why go to you?" Cap asked. "They were taking out folks with a lot higher power levels than Paulie Chase."

"They couldn't get close to Paulie without making an enemy of the entire Maggia," Benny said with a toothy grin. "They figured they needed an in . . . a way to catch him unawares, you know? And besides, with me on their side and Paulie gone, they figured I could be a powerful ally. I could work my way up the ranks, after all."

"No, you couldn't," Black Widow said.

Benny's grin faltered.

"What were Paulie's powers?" Cap asked.

"Regeneration, he called it," Benny said. "Not many knew about it. Only his inner circle."

"Looks like he trusted the wrong people, then," Cap said, looking at Benny with contempt.

"Wait a second," Black Widow said. "Paulie Chase could heal himself?"

"From any . . . you know, not mortal wound, yeah," Benny said. "Stabs, gunshot wounds . . . I mean, shoot the guy in the head, he's a freakin' goner, but you know what I mean."

"But you killed him," Cap said. "The puncture wound wouldn't have been fatal, and the amount of blood you drew wouldn't have killed him."

Benny looked at Cap right in the eye. "I didn't take just

one needle," he said. "I dug the thing into his throat and I *cut*. You think Paulie woulda let me live knowing I sold his blood? Get outta here. I had to kill him."

"For the payoff," Widow said.

"Gotta look out for number one," Benny said.

"And look where it got you," Cap said, grabbing Benny from Widow's hands and shoving him out the back door. A group of policemen were waiting, and one broke from the crowd, came over to them, and cuffed the mobster.

Cap and Black Widow walked back toward Widow's motorcycle, which was parked in front of the house next to Benny's. As Widow threw her leg over the side, motioning for Cap to join her, he instead watched as Benny was pushed into the squad car in front of them.

"What are you thinking?" Black Widow asked.

"Do you think Black Mamba really was going to heal Carmella?" he asked. "Contacting the mob to steal Paulie Chase's blood . . . that's a big risk. If she wasn't going to actually help, why do it?"

Widow stared at him, her eyes squinted in the daylight. "What if she was?"

"Huh?"

"What if she was going to help?" Black Widow asked. "She was still turning them into zombies. What, was she going to use a serum based on Paulie's powers to heal Carmella's body once she was turned into a lifeless puppet?"

"I don't know," Cap said.

"No matter what happens next, Anita and Carmella are in a better place," Black Widow said. "Everyone who was there is. What the Serpent Society was doing was unconscionable. You know that."

"I do," Cap said, nodded. He looked out at the sun, high in the sky, and sighed. "In all likelihood, she was going to use Paulie's blood for herself. Or the other members."

"Come on, Steve," Black Widow said, patting on the seat behind her. "Don't torture yourself over this stuff. We do what we can . . ."

"Because it's all we can do," Cap finished, walking over to her motorcycle. He wrapped his arms around her torso and they took off toward Brooklyn.

* * *

Elsewhere, in an otherwise empty wing of Metro-General Hospital, Tony Stark was lightly dozing in the waiting room. He wore a stylish suit, the shirt unbuttoned to his sternum, his legs crossed as he shifted in the uncomfortable chair.

He stirred awake, rubbing his eyes as Dr. Sternbaum, carrying a Stark Industries tablet, approached him. She wore a pristine white coat and glasses, which reflected the blue glow of the screen before her. Tony had handpicked her for this surgery, as she and her team were, to his knowledge, the best in the world.

Which meant that they were the best in the world.

"They're ready to see you, Mr. Stark," Sternbaum said.

"Are you not going to give me the *here's what you need to know*?" Tony said, motioning toward the tablet. "All the details folks normally don't listen to?"

Sternbaum smiled. "With the amount you're paying me by the hour, I thought it best not to waste your time. You know exactly what I'm going to say."

Tony nodded and reached out a hand. Sternbaum took it, giving it a single firm shake.

"Thanks, doc," Tony said, and walked toward the recovery room.

"If I may, Mr. Stark," Sternbaum said, as Tony continued to stride away from her. "Why these two young women?"

Tony shoved his hands in his pockets as he disappeared down the hall. "Because I lied to them. I figured the best thing I could do to make up for that was to make that lie come true."

Tony walked into the recovery room, which beeped with the dull, constant sounds of machinery. Both Anita and Carmella, dressed in hospital gowns, were hooked up to those machines, watching from their beds as Tony entered.

They were close enough to reach across the room and grab each other's hands, when they were strong enough to do so.

"I hope you don't mind a visitor," Tony said, standing before them.

"No one but you," Anita said, her voice low but strong. "I look like crap."

Tony nodded. "Yeah, maybe. At least you *both* look awful, though. There's that."

Carmella chuckled. Tony noted with satisfaction that her laugh sounded stronger now than it did even before the surgery. A good sign.

"Don't make her laugh," Anita scolded. "The surgeon said she shouldn't even be talking, really."

"Bah," Tony said, waving her off. "Bruce Banner and I designed those lungs ourselves. Those'll keep pumping long after the rest of your body is all withered and old."

Carmella gaped at him, mock offended.

"What? I'm just saying," Tony said. "The rest of your body came free. Sort of part of the whole *living* deal. You're now rocking with a multimillion dollar set of prosthetic lungs. I don't skimp on the details either. I'm willing to bet you could hold your breath under water for . . . let's say, ten minutes? At least? You could be a stunt woman. Boom. New career."

Carmella let out another chuckle, but Anita stared at him. Her eyes were sleepy, and her head was covered in bandages from where Dr. Sternbaum had operated. There were few doctors whom he trusted to perform the surgery needed to remove the mystical parasite from the girls' brains, but he knew Sternbaum could do it. After finishing up here, she would go to S.H.I.E.L.D.'s holding facility where the rest of the Serpent Society's lackeys were to perform the same surgery on all of them. All on Tony Stark's dime.

Sometimes, he just needed to feel like a hero.

Anita held his gaze. "Thank you."

"Don't thank me yet," Tony said. "You've got a long road ahead of you. I spoke to Maria Hill at S.H.I.E.L.D. Gave her the details on what you both did, how you helped stop the attack on the facility. She won't arrest you, but she does want to talk to you. And let me give you a friendly warning, as someone who talks to her on a regular basis, that can be all *types* of not fun."

"Seriously," Anita said, looking up at him. "I don't have the words to tell you how much this means to me."

Tony looked away from her and took a deep breath. "Well," he said, his voice thick. "Just goes to show you. Open a portal in the sky and unleash a giant stink monster, and you can get whatever you ask for. That's the lesson here, right?"

Anita smiled at Tony as he began to walk out of the room. "Where are you going?" she asked.

"I'll be back to visit before they release you," he said. "Barton has a little barbecue going on. It's a thing he does. It's no Tony Stark–level party, but he does his best. Maybe you two can come someday, once we're on the other side of all of this."

"Maybe," Anita said.

Offering a final nod to Anita and Carmella, Tony walked out of the recovery room, his head held high.

* * *

As the sun set over Clint Barton's apartment in Bed-Stuy, Brooklyn, the Avengers gathered with the building's residents in a circle, sitting on overturned crates, benches, and lawn chairs that they had assembled. Hawkeye had just finished grilling up ribs, which he passed down the line. Tony Stark, dressed in a suit, hurried to join the group as Thor moved to the center of the circle, clearing his throat.

"I'm here, I'm here," Tony said, sitting between Captain America and Black Widow. Bruce Banner reached into the cooler next to him and pulled out a bottle of water, tossing it to Tony, who caught it easily. He looked from Black Widow to Captain America to Thor, all of whom were in their uniforms. "This *is* a barbecue, right?"

"We're coming from a mission," Cap said, patting Tony on the back. "Tell you later."

Thor swept his crimson cape around, striking a pose. "No mission for me. I just look *great* in my armor."

"Can't argue there," Janet, Clint's neighbor said, as the group burst into laughter.

"Mom!" her daughter Emma cried. "Thor is trying to tell a story. Stop *flirting*."

As the laughter rose again and Janet brought her hand to her flushed face, Thor flipped Mjolnir in his hand and winked at her.

"And remember," Clint said, holding a warning finger up at Thor.

Thor nodded knowingly. "Of course, yes. Emma shall relate this tale to the young, fearful Timothy Hopper, so I will be sure to limit the blood, the violence, the horror, blah, blah, blah." He leaned toward Emma, grinning devilishly. "This is the tale . . . of the sky serpent, a beast of power and size unlike any this world has ever seen! Picture this, good people of Bed-Stuy. The Avengers lay defeated, all but for the mighty Thor, who single-handedly stood against the wicked demon—"

The other Avengers erupted in a chorus of boos, throwing chips and pieces of hamburger buns at Thor, who laughed heartily.

"He's lying, we all know he's lying," Hawkeye said over the laughter of his neighbors. "Let *me* tell you about the time I took down the Barglewarf, just across the street. Not even a *lick* of help from Thor."

As they laughed and playfully argued, Tony Stark stepped away from the crowd and walked toward the ledge. Captain America followed, finishing off his burger.

"Good food," Cap said.

Tony nodded. "Not many can barbecue like Barton. I'll give him that."

The two Avengers stood side by side, staring out at the night. It wasn't often that they could see stars over New York City, but on this late-summer night, the sky was bright with starlight.

"How are they?" Cap asked.

Tony let out a long breath. "I think they're going to be okay. Physically, at least."

"This kind of thing can change you, huh?" Cap said.

Tony turned to meet his blue eyes. "Yeah. It really can," he said. He looked over at his friends, laughing with Clint's neighbors, sharing stories and food. He couldn't help but smile. "Sometimes, maybe even for the better."

ACKNOWLEDGMENTS

I was in the middle of writing my first Marvel novel, *Iron Man: Mutually Assured Destruction*, when I learned that my next project would be this Avengers book. In *Iron Man*, I was greedy with my use of many super heroes that populate the Marvel Universe. I had cameos from most of the Avengers, just because I couldn't believe that I *could* do it—so, of course, I had to take advantage of it while I had the chance. For all I knew, it would be my only chance to write those magical words: "Captain America said."

But now, here I am, back again, and this time with the whole team. As I mentioned in my dedication, I am humbled to look back at the seemingly endless list of amazing creators who have contributed to the story of the Avengers. What amazes me so much about these writers, artists, colorists, letterers, editors, and designers is that they have created something more than just a team of super heroes with Captain America, Iron Man, Thor, Black Widow, Hawkeye, Hulk, and the rest of the characters that make up the many incarnations of this team. For me, the Avengers represent hope and humanity, even in the darkest times.

I wrote this book in 2016—a year that has been referred to, among other things, as a "dumpster fire." Now, I can't attest to exactly how dumpster fiery 2016 was as a whole, but I will say this . . . through the strangest and darkest times of the year, when I was struggling and lost, I found myself uplifted when I had to sit down in front of my laptop, open my manuscript, and ask myself, *What would Captain America do?*

For that respite in the midst of struggle, I have to again thank the creators who made the Avengers the symbols of hope that they are. In turn, I hope that those who read this novel might feel the same thing I did while writing it: the daring thought that even in the face of immense suffering or hardship, even when it seems that tomorrow isn't promised . . . that if we stick together and do what is right, everything might just be okay.

Pat Shand
January 2017

ABOUT THE AUTHOR

PAT SHAND writes comics (*Destiny NY, Robyn Hood, Van Helsing, Vampire Emmy & the Garbage Girl*), novels (*Marvel Iron Man: Mutually Assured Destruction, Marvel Avengers: The Serpent Society, Charmed: Social Medium, Charmed: Symphony for the Devil*), and more. He lives in New York with his fiancée Amy and their zoo of cats. Follow him @PatShand pretty much anywhere online. If you see him tweeting too much, remind him that he should be writing.